The Cape May Packet

The Black Buccaneer
Red Horse Hill
Away to Sea
Lumberjack
Who Rides in the Dark?
T-Model Tommy
Boy with a Pack
Clear for Action!
Blueberry Mountain
Shadow in the Pines
The Sea Snake
The Long Trains Roll
Jonathan Goes West
Behind the Ranges
River of the Wolves
Cedar's Boy
Whaler 'Round the Horn
Bulldozer

The Fish Hawk's Nest
Sparkplug of the Hornets
The Buckboard Stranger
Guns for the Saratoga
Sabre Pilot
Everglades Adventure
The Commodore's Cup
The Voyage of the Javelin
Wild Pony Island
Buffalo and Beaver
Snow on Blueberry Mountain
Phantom of the Blockade
The Muddy Road to Glory
Stranger on Big Hickory
A Blow for Liberty
Topsail Island Treasure
Keep 'Em Rolling
Lonesome End

STEPHEN W. MEADER

The Cape May Packet

ILLUSTRATED BY ROBERT FRANKENBERG

SOUTHERN SKIES

ISBN 978-1-931177- 62-7 cloth
ISBN 978-1-931177- 63-4 paperback

Library of Congress Catalog Card Number 78-82636

SOUTHERN SKIES

LITTLE ROCK, ARKANSAS
www.southernskies.com

Dedication

The republication of this book is dedicated with love to Lewis "Bud" Hyde---mentor, guide, confidante, friend for life--- by Jerry Atchley.

The longer I live in Cape May County, down at the southern tip of New Jersey, the more I am fascinated by its history. Many of my neighbors bear the names of the early settlers who came down from Long Island or New England for the whaling. And when, for some reason, the whales departed from the area, these hardy folk stayed on, to live by fishing or farming.

A surprising number of men, especially from Lower Township, were in the piloting business. As the commerce of the port of Philadelphia grew, skilled men were needed to bring the great merchant ships in safely and navigate the treacherous waters of Delaware Bay and River.

Shipbuilding was another of the county's trades, and many a fast sloop and schooner was launched here. After the Revolution, some enterprising skippers used such craft as packet boats, carrying meat, vegetables, and other produce from Cape May to Philadelphia. And on the return voyage, in summer weather, they brought passengers who wanted to enjoy the sea bathing. Most people preferred the water journey to rattling over sandy roads in the stage. They came from Baltimore and Washington, as well as Philadelphia, and made Cape Island America's first great beach resort.

When the War of 1812 began, Cape May County bore

the brunt of the British raids, sent ashore from the fleet that blockaded Delaware Bay. It is this period of trouble and danger that forms the background of my story.

Will Hand was typical of the boys who lived through those times—half farmer, half sailor, and all clear Yankee grit. The day of the sailing packets, such as the *Fair Molly*, was destined to be brief. By 1816 steamboats began plying the Delaware, and it was the steam side-wheelers that brought thousands of summer people down in the 1840's and 1850's, giving Cape May the charming Victorian look it still wears today.

The Cape May Packet

One

The sun beat down on Market Street wharf, and young Will Hand took off his hat to let the breeze cool his forehead.

"Too bad," he thought to himself. "A fine July day, hot an' clear, when you'd think half o' Philadelphia would want to go ocean bathing. An' not a passenger in sight!"

Beside him the sloop *Fair Molly* lay moored to the dockside. With her mainsail down, she looked broad-beamed and comfortable, like a country housewife in her kitchen. Only an experienced sailor would have noticed the grace in her lines, telling of speed as well as seaworthiness.

Will watched the drays and farmers' carts rumbling by over the cobbles of the waterfront, carrying produce to Dock Street Market. His father's own cargo of fruit and vegetables had been unloaded there early that morning. Now Captain Ezra Hand was up at the countinghouse, and Will had been left to look after the sloop.

Every few minutes he let out a shout. "Here you are! Packet for Cape May! Fastest way to the beaches an' most comfortable! No jouncin' over the roads. No stops to change horses. Just a nice, pleasant overnight sail, with a good dinner served on board!"

Out of breath, he took a bandanna from his pocket and mopped his face. Then, hopefully, he looked up along Front Street to see if anyone had heard him.

A black head appeared above the galley hatch aboard the *Fair Molly*. It was Hannibal, cook and able seaman.

"How 'bout it, boy?" he asked grumpily. "Goin' to have anybody to eat my grub?"

"Doesn't look like it. But there's time enough yet 'fore the tide turns. You go ahead an' cook your chowder."

Hannibal retreated once more, and Will watched a squad of soldiers tramping south toward a troop ship, with muskets on their shoulders. That was the trouble with the packet-boat business, he knew. The war! It had started two years before, in 1812, much to the disgust of most Jerseymen like his father. Ever since, the British had kept up a tight blockade of the Delaware, so that there were no merchant ships entering or leaving. Before the war, Ezra Hand had been one of the best pilots on the bay, and the *Fair Molly* had been a pilot boat. Now her skipper had to make a living by carrying cargoes and passengers between Cape May and Philadelphia.

Will had been fourteen when the *Constitution* sank the *Guerrière*, and it looked then as if the war would soon be over. Then, more than a year later, Commodore Perry had thoroughly whipped the British fleet on Lake Erie. But along the Atlantic Coast the blockade grew ever harder

12

to break. Even Stephen Decatur, commanding the port of New York, was completely bottled up. The young nation was fighting for its life, and all good Americans had now come to support the struggle.

It was nearing eleven o'clock when Will saw his father's rugged figure coming down the waterfront. Just as he turned at the head of the dock, a carriage appeared. It was drawn by two handsome horses and driven by a coachman.

As the horses picked their way over the cobbles, Will's hopes rose again. Surely the three occupants of the elegant vehicle were looking for the sloop, so he raised his voice once more.

"Right here she lies! The Cape May packet—quickest way to Cape Island an' the ocean bathing!"

Ezra Hand heard the different sound as the hoofs clop-clopped on the planking of the dock. He turned and raised a hand in greeting to the occupants of the carriage.

"You folks lookin' to travel on the packet?" he asked.

The coachman brought his team to a stop, and the well-dressed gentleman nodded to the captain.

"What time do you sail?" he inquired.

"Tide'll turn in about ten minutes," Will's father answered. "That's when we'll be startin'. I reckon you an' the ladies might like to have a look at the cabin."

As they stepped down from the carriage, Will saw a lady in expensive-looking clothes and a very pretty girl, perhaps a year younger than himself.

"Yes," said the man. "We'll inspect the quarters before we decide."

Proudly Will gave them a hand down to the well-

scrubbed deck of the sloop. "The *Fair Molly*'s not so fancy," he told them, "but we keep her clean. The cabin's right aft, here. Nice, soft mattresses on the bunks an' a screen to separate the ladies an' gentlemen."

The woman cast a searching eye about the cabin and felt the mattresses. "You know, James," she remarked to her husband, "it *is* clean, and it smells sweet—much better

than that dreadful inn where we stopped last year."

The man nodded. "If you're satisfied," he said, "we may as well have Perkins bring our luggage aboard. How much do you charge, young man?"

Will blushed. "Right now," he said, "with the war an' all, it's four dollars for each passenger. But that includes meals, an' I guarantee you'll like 'em."

"Very well, here's your twelve dollars. I'm James Perry, of Spruce Street. This is Mrs. Perry, and here's my daughter, Kate. I've heard of the *Fair Molly*, and I take it your name must be Hand?"

"I'm Will Hand. My dad is Cap'n Ezra Hand, the owner of the packet."

Within a few minutes the coachman had carried half a dozen bags down to the cabin and taken his leave. Mr. Perry and his daughter came on deck as Will was casting off the mooring ropes. Then he ran to the halyards to hoist the big gaff mainsail. And just as the tide began to ebb, the *Fair Molly* swung out into the current.

Mr. Perry was conversing with Ezra Hand, aft by the tiller, and Mrs. Perry had stayed in the cabin. It was the girl who came forward to talk to Will while he hoisted the jib. She was even prettier than he had realized. She had flashing dark eyes, and her copper-colored hair was blowing in the breeze.

"So many ships tied up at their wharves!" she remarked. "The poor old Delaware seems quite empty, doesn't it?"

"That's right," Will told her. "It's been this way ever since the war began. That brig over yonder by the Jersey shore is a Navy patrol ship, an' she's probably the only squarerigger we'll see today."

"How long do you expect the trip will take us?" asked the girl.

Will looked aloft at the draw of the big mainsail. "Well," he replied, "with the tide to help an' a fair wind, we ought to be down into the bay by six o'clock. Then we'll be slowed down after the tide turns. I reckon Dad expects to reach the cape before daylight tomorrow."

"Really?" she asked in surprise. "It's the first time we've gone down by water. Mother doesn't mind the jolting of the coaches so much, but she says all the beds at the inns have bugs! Do you live at Cape May?"

"Not right on Cape Island but there in the county. Our place is in Cold Spring, a little way north."

"My," she said with a sigh, "it must be fun to live so near the bathing beaches. Do you swim there often?"

Will's face reddened. "I swim, all right," he said, "but generally in the creek or the bay. I don't own one o' those fancy bathing outfits the visitors wear on the beach."

Kate Perry seemed amused. "That's a good enough reason," she told him with a laugh. "I hope you can come down anyway while we're there. We'll be stopping at Mr. Hughes's hotel."

They were interrupted by Hannibal, who emerged from the galley and pounded on a large pan with a wooden spoon.

"Chowder's ready!" he announced in a deep singsong baritone. "Bes' eat it while it's hot."

"Oh, dear!" said the girl. "I don't seem to be very hungry yet."

"That's all right," Will told her. "Chowder tastes better the longer it stands. Anyhow, we're comin' to the booms in a minute. You can see how Dad steers her through."

In the last hour the sloop had sailed well below the city and was now approaching a narrow part of the river opposite Hog Island. Ezra Hand stood up, watching the current ahead. He waited for the right moment and swung the tiller hard over as he slacked the sheet. Obediently the *Fair Molly* made a turn to port, and suddenly, under her lee, there appeared a line of huge logs, chained end to end. Fifty yards away on the starboard side was a similar log boom, and the sloop sailed between them for two or three minutes.

"All right," Will told his companion, "here's the end o' the lower boom. We made it an' never touched a log!"

"That's wonderful!" Kate exclaimed. "I'm sure a British frigate would get all tangled up if she tried it."

Will nodded. "That's true enough. An' there are big guns in the forts, both sides o' the river. You'd better eat some o' Hannibal's chowder now, or you'll hurt his feelin's!"

❊   ❊   ❊

It was an hour later, and the sloop was below Chester, when the Perry family came on deck again. This time Kate's mother was with her. They sat in the cockpit in the shade of the mainsail and admired the green shores of the river.

"This seems like a very comfortable little vessel," Mrs. Perry commented. "What's your name, young man, if I may ask?"

"His name's Willing Hand," Ezra put in with a chuckle. "That was his ma's idea. But most folks just call him Will."

"How quaint!" said the lady. "Willing Hand!"

"Oh," Will's father said, "it don't stop there. His older sister's named Faithful, an' the youngest girl's Loving Hand—Lovey for short."

When the smiles had subsided, James Perry spoke up. "You seem to know the Delaware well, Captain," he said. "Do you make this trip fairly often?"

"Generally a couple o' times a week in the summer," the skipper replied. "Come winter, there isn't much cargo except mitten goods an' such. An' o' course nobody wants to go sea-bathin' in the cold months. I've only been runnin' the packet here since the war started. 'Fore that I was a Delaware Bay pilot," he added proudly.

"What did you mean by 'mitten goods'?" Kate asked, full of curiosity.

"Well, our Cape May womenfolks have always been great knitters," Ezra Hand told her. "They spin their own wool an' knit mittens, stockin's, scarves—all sorts o' warm things. There's a pretty fair market for 'em up in the city. More'n one farmer's been helped through the winter by the cash his wife's knittin' brings in."

The tide began to slacken about four in the afternoon, but the wind still held fair from the west. The *Fair Molly* kept on her course, making five or six knots, and ahead they could see the channel curving southeastward.

"Head o' the bay," Ezra grunted. "We're right on time so far."

The water had become a little more choppy here in the widening estuary. Mrs. Perry seemed to feel the slight rocking of the sloop.

"I think," she said, "I'd better go below and lie down. No supper, please. I'll just have a cup of tea."

Kate went down to the cabin with her. When she returned, she shook her head. "Poor Mother!" she said to Will. "The least bit of motion makes her sure she's going to be seasick."

The sun was close to setting when they sighted an armed

cutter tacking up the bay. She flew the American flag, so Ezra Hand steered near enough to hail her.

"Any news from below?" he asked, after giving the name of the sloop.

"Yes—we sighted two British men-o'-war inside the capes," came the answer. "You better heave to till morning."

"Thanks," called the captain with a grin. "Sounds like good advice."

But an hour passed and dusk approached, and the *Fair Molly* still sailed on.

"What do you plan to do?" James Perry asked. "Shouldn't we drop anchor?"

"Nope," Ezra replied. "Don't intend to. You see I know every inch o' the bay—both shores, too. I can get you safe to Cape May, but I won't need daylight to do it. The British are the ones that'll have to heave to. You go ahead down to the cabin an' have a good night's rest."

The Philadelphia man stopped worrying and began to smile. "I'm sure you're right, Captain," he said. "Good night!"

Will came aft to join his father. "What about running lights?" he asked. "You want 'em on tonight?"

"No. I'd rather run dark. No danger o' meetin' any river traffic below here, an' if the British are prowlin' up into the bay, I'd just as leave they didn't see us."

"What do you think of our passengers, Dad? They seem to me like nice, friendly folks, spite of all their money."

It wasn't too dark for Will to see a smile on his father's face. "Yep," he replied. "I noticed you found the young lass friendly enough."

Will curled up on the forward deck and slept for a few hours. When he awoke, the lapping of the water under the forefoot had changed its sound. He knew the tide was starting to turn again and would soon be running toward the sea. Also his clothes had a damp feel, and his muscles were stiff. He could no longer see any stars overhead.

"Fog comin' in pretty soon," his father commented when Will went aft to join him. "Take the tiller an' give me a couple o' minutes to stretch my legs."

Shortly he returned to the helm. "We're off the Cohansey now," he said, "an' I'd better pick up some oysters for the hotels. Watch the boom when I come about."

Within a quarter of an hour, the sloop was making her way up the channel of a broad creek on the New Jersey shore. A dozen oyster boats loomed ghostly at their moorings, and a crude pier thrust out from the land.

"Who's there?" A voice hailed them from the wharf.

"Cap'n Hand, o' the *Fair Molly*," Will's father replied. "No need to holler so loud. I've got passengers asleep in the cabin. Thought I'd see if you could sell me a barrel o' fresh oysters."

"Sure," said the man. "Come alongside an' I'll roll 'em down from the shed."

As Will sprang to the wharf and moored the sloop to a bollard, he could hear the rumble as the oysterman rolled a barrel along the planking.

"These good an' fresh?" Ezra Hand asked.

"Yep. Dredged 'em myself this afternoon, an' they're big 'uns. Have to charge ye two dollars a barrel for extra fine Cohanseys."

Among the three of them, they managed to transfer the

heavy barrel to the deck without too much noise. It must have weighed close to two hundred pounds. Then Will's father paid the oysterman, and the sloop made sail once more. By midnight they were out in Delaware Bay again.

"That's a lot o' money to charge for oysters!" Ezra Hand grumbled. "Must come to half a cent apiece!"

"Oh, well," his son told him, "Ellis Hughes'll be glad to pay it. Those customers o' his love to eat, an' he feeds 'em well."

Two

As the captain had predicted, fog shrouded the waters of the lower bay before daylight. This was all in the *Fair Molly*'s favor, for the British patrol ships would be forced to stay at anchor. The sloop, on the other hand, made her way down the shore without trouble.

At six o'clock Will heard a clatter of pans in the galley. Not long after that James Perry came on deck, yawning and rubbing his eyes.

"Why," he exclaimed, "you're sailing along as if you could see where you're going!"

"That's true enough," said the former pilot cheerfully. "Right now we're half a mile west o' Green Creek. I'm stayin' close to shore in case the fog lifts."

"It's startin' to break already, Dad," Will called from the foredeck. "See the sun comin' through, over the cape?"

A stronger breeze was blowing from the west now, and

the morning tide was coming in from the sea. The cross chop made the sloop's motion more noticeable.

"My wife may be feeling seasick," said Mr. Perry. "I'd better go and look after her."

As he went to the cabin, his daughter came on deck, looking fresh and bright-eyed.

"Good morning!" she called. "I had a wonderful sleep. When do we reach Cape May?"

"We'll be landing pretty quick," the captain told her. "But it won't be at Cape Island. If we tried to sail around the point, there'd be trouble from the frigate out yonder."

Looking where he pointed, Will and the girl could make out the dim outline of a big ship through the thinning fog, perhaps a mile to windward.

"We'll put into Cox Hall Creek," Captain Hand explained to Kate. "There we'll be well hid, an' it won't take long to run you down to Cape Island in the wagon."

Shortly he shifted the tiller and told Will to stand by the halyards. As they swung to the left, a wooded bluff appeared ahead of them. The entrance to the creek was so well hidden that Kate Perry didn't see it at first.

"We'll run aground!" she cried in alarm.

"Take up the centerboard!" Ezra Hand ordered crisply. "When you've made it fast, stand by to drop the mainsail."

Kate's father came out of the cabin just then. He stared in amazement as Will cranked a small windlass on the side of the narrow, boxlike arrangement in the middle of the cockpit. Peering into the centerboard well, he saw a wooden plank rising toward the top. Will jammed a long spike through a hole, and the plank was held firmly in place.

"Say!" he exclaimed. "If that's what I think, it's quite a contraption!"

"It's what they call a leeboard or centerboard," the captain told him. "Acts like a keel when it's let down. This sloop's shallow draft—only about four feet, so she can get into the inlets. But out in deep water, she needs a keel to keep her from driftin' sideways. A couple o' Cape May County men named Swain invented this gadget, an' it works fine. The *Fair Molly*'s one o' the first boats that's got it. Ain't even been patented yet."

The sloop was in the mouth of the inlet now, and Will had lowered the big mainsail. He took a long pole and thrust it into the mud alongside, helping propel the craft forward. Within a minute or two, she was alongside a tiny dock on the shore of a little cove, completely hidden from the outer world.

"All right, Will," his father commanded. "Get down to the farm and bring the horse an' wagon. I'll take care o' things here. Step lively, now!"

Will scrambled up the path to the top of the bluff and set off at a steady trot along the Town Bank trail. It was more than two miles to the Hand farm in Cold Spring, but he was a good runner. He was scarcely out of breath when he jogged into the dooryard.

"Hi, Ma!" he panted. "We're back."

Martha Hand was a tall woman, gaunt from hard work but still handsome in a stern, Presbyterian way. She smiled from the doorway at her son.

"Breakfast's 'most ready, Willing," she said. "Where's your pa?"

"Back in Cox Hall Creek. We had to put in there 'cause o' the British. Got some passengers for Cape Island, so he sent me to fetch the wagon."

His mother looked disappointed. "Well," she remarked, "I hope Ezra gets here pretty soon. There's farm work that needs doing."

Will grinned to himself as he put the harness on Bess, the old bay mare. Martha Hand had been a Corson before her marriage—a farm-bred girl. The sea was a foreign element to her, and it was hard for her to understand her husband's love of salt water. Will could sympathize with both his parents' points of view. But he knew they loved each other, and their differences never cut too deep.

"Giddap, Bess!" he called, slapping the reins on the mare's rump. The light wagon rattled out of the yard, and he set off up the old Cape Road.

The sun had been up well over an hour when he halted the rig at the top of the bluff. Will was hungry, but he knew he would get little chance to eat this morning. As soon as he reached the sloop, his father called him to help carry the Perrys' bags up the path. But as he passed the galley, Hannibal quietly placed a "fried pie" in his hand. It was a doughnut-like object with a center of dried apple soaked in molasses—a really delicious morsel that he finished in three bites.

He grinned at the cook in gratitude, then picked up some pieces of luggage and set about carrying them to the top of the bluff. His father, leading their passengers, was already halfway up. They stowed the bags under the two seats and helped Mr. and Mrs. Perry and Kate to clamber aboard. The ladies shared the back seat, and James Perry took his place in front.

"You'll drive, Will," said Ezra Hand. "I'll walk home, soon as Hannibal an' I get the sloop snugged down. Come home as quick as you can."

They drove along the top of the bluff to a trail that led inland toward the Cape Road.

"Well," said Mr. Perry contentedly, "it's a fine morning, and we had a good breakfast. That man of yours is quite a cook. Do you suppose your father would be willing to sell him if the price were big enough?"

Will chuckled. "He couldn't if he wanted to, sir," he answered. "Hannibal's been free since before I was born. One time he used to cook for Ephraim Mills, at the old hotel, but he says he likes boats better."

"How far is it to the beach?" Kate asked. "I don't want to miss the morning bathing time."

"It's close to five miles—not more'n an hour's ride," Will told her. "Ladies get to bathe from ten till eleven, so you'll be in plenty o' time."

Once on the harder surface of the old Cape Road, Bess's gait changed to a trot, and the wagon moved faster. Will had to slow down when they approached the narrow wooden bridge across Island Creek. The mare planted her feet gingerly on the rickety planks, and they went creaking over.

"There," said Will, "we're in Cape Island now. Right yonder is Eph Mills's hotel, an' on down toward the beach is Ellis Hughes's."

The hotel, when they reached it, was a frame structure

about fifty feet square, dotted with small windows. The Perrys, who had been there before, didn't seem taken aback by its barnlike appearance. In fact, the wagon had barely stopped when Kate sprang out over the wheel and raced toward the doorway where Mrs. Hughes stood waiting.

"You see," the girl cried gaily, "we did come back, war or no war!"

"Glad you're here safe, dearie," the innkeeper's wife replied. "Not so many folks are here this time, but the surf-bathing's as good as ever 'twas."

Will got down, assisted Mrs. Perry out of the wagon, then helped to carry the bags into the hotel.

"My dad picked up some oysters last night in the Cohansey," he told Mrs. Hughes as he was leaving. "If you reckon you can use 'em, we'll bring some down, maybe this afternoon."

"I'll be glad to have oysters," she answered. "With the British standin' offshore all the time, mighty few oystermen come down this way."

Will drove back to the farm in the midmorning heat. He wished he could be with Kate, enjoying the cool surf, but he knew there was no chance. There were strict rules forbidding men and women to bathe together, so he'd have to wait for a swim in the creek. Right now there would probably be farm chores to occupy him.

He was drowsy when old Bess pulled into the yard, and the wagon's sudden stop shook him awake.

Lovey was at the well, trying to draw a bucket of water. "Lazybones!" she called to him. "Come an' help me with this heavy thing!"

He grinned as he sauntered over. A hand on the weighted end of the well sweep brought the dripping bucket up in a hurry, and he took it off the hook, walking with it to the kitchen.

"Here I am, Ma," he announced. "Anything to eat? I never got any breakfast—only one fried pie Hannibal gave me."

"Ezra!" she called. "You trying to starve this boy?"

There was no reply, for his father was out in the barn. Will had scarcely had time to wash his hands when his mother set a plate of fried eggs on the table, along with bread, butter, jam, and a pitcher of milk.

"Busy, are they, down at the hotel?" she inquired.

"I reckon not," said Will. "Looked to me like the Perrys would have the place mostly to themselves."

She nodded. "It's the war," she replied. "Bad business for everybody."

By the time the boy had finished eating, his father came into the kitchen. "I doubt if the Hugheses can use a whole barrel of oysters," he said. "Martha, why don't you ask around amongst the neighbors—find out if anybody wants some?"

"All right," she answered. "An' we can keep a few ourselves for a nice stew. You plan to hoe that corn today?"

"I'll get to it," Ezra told her, without much enthusiasm. "First, though, we've got to fetch a few things from the sloop an' get 'em delivered. There's more cash money in that than there is in hoein' corn."

This was good news to Will, who shared his father's feeling about farm work. But his father hadn't finished yet.

"Will," he said, "you go saddle the colt an' ride up to

Swain's store, at Fishin' Creek. Tell Joe Swain to drive down an' get the molasses an' women's shoes he ordered. It's all right to let him know where we've got the sloop if he don't tell anyone else. I'll be there when you get back."

Will was glad to hear this order, for the black colt was his special pride and joy. A chance to ride him was more than he had expected, and he hurried to saddle up.

"Black Prince," as the colt was called, hadn't had any exercise for the past three days and was hard to handle. Once Will got the bridle on and the girth pulled tight, he talked soothingly to the black and patted his silky neck.

"Easy now, boy," he said. "I'll let you out once we're on the road, an' you'll have all the run you want."

He swung into the saddle and got his feet in the stirrups before Prince realized what was happening. Then the colt made a playful buck or two, snorted, and began to run. Will turned him north on the dirt road and let him have his head.

In the July heat, the young horse was soon satisfied to drop his headlong gallop to an easy canter. They had traveled about three miles up the Cape Road when the colt shied suddenly. Something had scuttled up the bank into the brush. All Will saw was a movement of leaves among the shadbush and bayberry, and he heard no sound. But he was almost sure the creature that had vanished was human.

"Hey!" he called. "Who's there?"

No answer came back, and he rode on. A few minutes later they passed a dilapidated roadside tavern with a swinging sign that badly needed painting. The dim in-

scription read: "Ichabod Leech. Refreshment for man and beast."

"Hm," muttered Will under his breath. "Refreshment, eh? From all I hear, the food an' drink are as poor as the beds."

A tall flagpole stood in front of the inn, but it occurred

to Will that he had never seen a flag flying from it. That fact seemed to bear out the story he had heard—that the Leeches were something less than patriotic.

He rode on till he reached the sandy crossroad that led to Fishing Creek. Joseph Swain's store was at the edge of the little settlement, and shortly Will was tying the colt to the hitching rail in front of the place.

He went up the porch steps and entered the store. It was dark inside after the bright sunshine, and he had to pause a moment to let his eyes adjust. The interior was full of boxes and barrels, tools stacked in the corners, and boots, oilskins, hams, and strings of onions hanging from the rafters. There was a fascinating smell of spices and coffee and of the great round cheeses that stood on the counter.

"Anybody here?" he called, and Mr. Swain in person came out of the back room.

"Oh," he said, "it's Will Hand. You're back from the city, I take it."

"Yes, sir. My dad wanted you to know he's got the things you ordered. The sloop's hid in Cox Hall Creek if you'd like to bring your wagon down."

"Can't make it today, but the stuff'll keep. Tell Ezra if he'll take it home, I'll come to your place an' pick it up tomorrow mornin'."

Will paid him a penny for a stick of black licorice and bade the storekeeper good-by. Since his father had said he would be at the sloop, there was no point in riding home. He guided the colt into a narrow path that led southward along the bay shore. Part of the way the trail skirted the marsh, but soon it climbed a bluff into the woods.

As he rode, Will chewed on his licorice stick, paying little attention to what was around him. But the sudden snapping of a stick, off to the left of the path, made him fully alert. He reined in the nervous young horse and sat staring into the underbrush. Some distance away a human figure broke cover and ran off among the trees. But before it vanished, Will got an impression of a torn homespun shirt and a shock of unkempt black hair.

That was the second time in a day that someone had run at his approach. Was he being spied on? The idea stayed with him all the way to the little cove where the *Fair Molly* lay concealed.

Three

It was something of a relief to find the sloop all safe at her
moorings. Will saw the farm wagon, with old Bess between
the shafts, standing at the top of the bluff, while down in
the cockpit of the *Fair Molly* his father was talking to
Hannibal.

He tied Prince to the tail of the wagon and ran down
the slope. As soon as he had delivered Swain's message,
the three of them began carrying cargo up the path. The
barrel of oysters was the heaviest item, but once Hannibal had it on his shoulder, he clambered steadily to the
top. Ezra and Will followed with smaller kegs and bundles.
When everything was stowed in the wagon, they stood
there panting in the heat.

"Might get a thunder-gust out o' this 'fore night," said
the skipper, casting a weather eye aloft. "Hannibal, you
stay with the sloop. Got enough vittles to keep you?"

The big man's teeth showed in a grin. "Don't fret about

me, boss," he replied. "It's a mighty poor cook that can't feed hisself!"

Will got into the seat beside his father, and they set out for home, with the colt following meekly behind.

"Dad," Will asked, "do you know the Leech family by sight?"

"You mean the folks that keep the tavern? I've only set eyes on 'em once or twice. Surly cuss, that Ichabod Leech. They've got no time for the packet boats 'cause they figure we take business from the stage line. They're newcomers to the county an' don't seem to have made friends with any o' the neighbors. Some say they're really on the British side in the war. What made you ask?"

"Oh, nothin' much. I wondered if you knew what the son looked like. Somebody was spyin' on me, back in the woods, an' I thought it might be young Leech."

"That'd be Ferdinand Leech—Ferd, they call him. Pale-lookin' feller a bit older'n you? Hair black an' straggly, an' a sort o' ferrety face?"

"Could be," said Will. "All I saw was his back when he ran off. But the hair sure sounds right."

Ezra Hand frowned. "Wonder what he'd want to follow you for," he mused. "You suppose he might be tryin' to find out where we'd hid the sloop?"

"I don't know," Will answered. "But I'd feel a heap better if the militia would sort o' keep an eye on their place."

It was well along in the afternoon when the wagon reached Atlantic Hall, as Hughes was beginning to call his hotel. With the help of the proprietor, they unloaded his provisions, and Ezra Hand received his pay. Will looked around, hoping for a glimpse of Kate Perry, but all the guests were reading or napping and out of sight.

"Dad," he said, "do you mind if I stay a little while longer? I've got the colt here, an' I can ride home."

His father looked at him with a twinkle in his eye. "All right," he replied. "Just so you're home in time for supper an' the chores. I'll tell your ma you had to do an errand for me an' won't mention it was this mornin'."

After the wagon had left, Will wandered down to the beach and amused himself by pitching clamshells at a mark in the sand. He knew the ladies' afternoon bathing time was half-past four, so there would be a few minutes to wait.

When he had first visited Cape Island, ten years before, it had seemed a long way from the hotel to the water. Now he could see the distance was shorter, for the ocean was gradually eating away the bank above the beach. Once he had seen Captain Stephen Decatur measuring the number of feet from the hotel to the high-tide mark. The famous naval hero was a regular visitor there, and Will had heard him say that the sea was stealing an average of ten feet of beach a year.

"Some day," he had told Mr. Hughes, "you'll have to move your house, unless you want the waves to break over it."

Promptly at four-thirty, several female figures came from the hotel, and Will withdrew to a respectful distance. He recognized Kate and her mother but didn't try to speak to them. Gentlemen were not supposed to watch the ladies at these times.

Will thought Kate looked quite fetching in her bathing

dress. It was of black wool material and reached to the ankles. It had long sleeves and a little frilled collar. She also wore black stockings and slippers, and over her coppery curls was a bathing hat. She raced ahead of the others and entered the low surf with little squeals of delight.

One of the other ladies saw Will standing there, and though he couldn't hear what she said, it must have been highly disapproving. He turned and made his way off as fast as possible. Five minutes later he was riding Black Prince homeward.

Clouds were towering in the west when he took the saddle off the colt and put him in his stall. As his father had foretold, there was a thunderstorm coming up, and Will was glad to get inside the house before it rained.

The distant rumbling became much louder, and by the time supper was ready, the lightning flashes were all around them. The girls were sent running upstairs to shut the windows. Martha Hand, who was in deadly fear of electrical storms, hurried to hide her sewing needles under a pillow and shut herself in the bedroom. She was firm in her belief that any small object made of steel would "draw lightning."

In the kitchen, Will and his father served themselves and ate calmly through all the commotion. A wind had come with the rain. It blew in fierce gusts for a few minutes, then subsided, and the storm passed on to the eastward, leaving a refreshing coolness behind it.

"All clear, Martha," called Ezra Hand. "Better come out now, while there's still food to eat."

✿   ✿   ✿

The next morning was fine and bright, with less humidity in the air. But, as Will had feared, the corn hoeing could be put off no longer. With a jug of cold water from the well, he set off for the upper field as soon as he had had breakfast. It was still only seven o'clock.

Like his father, Will was more seaman than farmer. But he knew they needed the corn to keep the stock through the winter, so he endured the hard, monotonous job. Some time in the middle of the morning, he paused to lean on his hoe and mop his forehead. Over on the road he heard a thud of hoofs and a creaking of wheels and was amazed to see old Bess coming at a gallop. His father was plying the whip from the seat of the light wagon.

Something, Will knew, must be very wrong, for he had never known Ezra Hand to use the whip. Hastily he picked up his jug, now nearly empty, and started for the house at a run. When he reached the dooryard, the mare was standing between the shafts, head down and breathing heavily. His father must have hurried into the house.

At the kitchen door Will met him coming out, and he had the big old ten-gauge shotgun in his hand.

"We've got trouble, boy!" he said gruffly. "Somebody cut the sloop's moorin's. Must ha' been before daylight, when Hannibal was asleep. He felt the side scrape against the bank an' woke up in time to keep her from driftin' out into the bay."

"Any idea who it was?"

"Can't be sure, but I'd say it was some skunk that don't like packet boats. Your guess is as good as mine."

Will nodded. He didn't say so, but his thoughts went

back to the slinking figure of Ferd Leech.

"I'm takin' the gun up to Hannibal," his father said.

"Old Bess looks mighty tired," Will commented. "Wouldn't you rather have me saddle the colt an' ride up there?"

Ezra Hand looked at the sweating mare and finally agreed. "Don't take all day," he cautioned. "You've still got to hoe corn."

The heavy gun was an awkward thing to carry, but fortunately Prince wasn't inclined to be skittish that morning, and Will made the trip to Cox Hall Creek without trouble. He tied the colt to a sapling at the top of the bluff and went down the path to the cove. It was quiet there. A cardinal sang sweetly in the trees across the creek, and the only other sound was the drowsy buzz of flies, down near the water.

Hannibal came out on deck at Will's approach and took the shotgun in his hands with a grave face.

"You know how to load it an' shoot it, don't you?" Will asked.

"Yes, I do. Jes' hope I don't have to use it. Killin' folks ain't much fun."

Will gave him the shot pouch and powder flask and watched the cook proceed to load the weapon. It was fairly obvious he had handled firearms before. The cut mooring line had been neatly spliced during the morning, Will saw.

"All right," he told Hannibal, "sleep with one eye open tonight, in case they come back. This time they might do somethin' worse."

"Don' fret yourself, boy. They won't catch me nappin' twice. You had your dinner? I got some nice hot chowder made."

Gratefully Will accepted a bowl of it, steaming hot from the galley stove. For a while he ate without talking. Then he rose regretfully.

"Got to get home," he told the cook. "Dad'll skin me if I don't get back to that cornfield."

He had ridden only half a mile when he heard a pounding of hoofs coming down the Cape Road. Will pulled over to the side and looked over his shoulder. The man on the lathered horse was Jesse Springer, an officer of the militia company that had its headquarters in Green Creek. He reined in as he drew abreast.

"You ridin' home?" he asked. "Stop at Corsons' an' Fosters', will you? Tell 'em the British have come ashore at Fishin' Creek. Four boatloads of 'em. They're takin' all the cattle they can get. We'll meet at Swain's store an' move from there."

Without more words he kicked his horse into action and galloped on. Will swung off to the left at the next crossroad and rode swiftly to the two farms Springer had mentioned. They were only a quarter of a mile apart, and both on his way home.

It was noon now, so the men had come in from the fields. At each place Will needed only a moment to deliver his message, and almost before he was out of the yard, the young militiamen were running to saddle their horses. How he wished he was old enough to be one of them!

Summonses of this kind were all too common in those

days. It seemed as if every ship that wanted fresh meat sent boats ashore to rob the farms. They never raided far inland, so up to now the Hand place had escaped. But it was their friends along the bay who suffered.

The skirmishes between landing parties and militia were not always one-sided. More than once the redcoats had turned tail at the sight of determined riflemen lying in wait for them. And though the ships' boats usually mounted small cannon, some of the militia companies could more than match them with artillery of their own.

The difficulty was that the Americans had to work their farms. It was impossible to patrol the shore day and night, and too often the raiders were able to make off with their booty before the Yankees could be gathered for defense.

Will reached home while the family was still at table, but he was too excited to eat. He unsaddled the colt and put him in his stall, then hurried in to bring his father the news.

"You didn't see the British boats, did you?" Ezra Hand asked.

"No—I reckon they landed farther up—Fishin' Creek, Jesse Springer said. So I guess the *Fair Molly*'s safe enough. I gave Hannibal the gun an' saw him load it."

His father was scowling as he paced the floor. "Durn robbers!" he muttered. "Wish there was more I could do to get back at 'em!"

"I know," said Will. "Long as they keep their ships in the bay, there isn't much anybody can do by water. They've sure finished the packet-boat business."

"Well, I'll think on what to do," his father told him. "But

meantime, there's nothin' to keep you from hoein' corn. Better get started."

It was somewhat cooler that afternoon. There was a breeze coming down across the woods and fields from the northwest, though it was still very hot.

He had been at work only a few minutes when he heard it—a faint crackling sound borne on the breeze. For a moment he thought it sounded like a distant brush fire. Then he knew it was the crackle of musketry. Somewhere a few miles north on the bay shore, there was a fight in progress!

He leaned on his hoe and listened. The sound died out, then came again on the wind. After a few minutes he could no longer hear it, and he went slowly back to his hoeing. Then suddenly came the dull boom of a cannon, unmistakable in the stillness.

Will could stand it no longer. He ran for the house as fast as he could go. He was out of breath when he reached the kitchen door.

"Where's Dad?" he demanded of his sister Faithful.

She looked scared. "Gone to Fishing Creek," she answered. "Ma couldn't make him stay home. Are they fighting up there?"

"Yes," he told her. "Anyhow, I heard some shootin'. Where's Ma?"

Faith pointed toward the bedroom. "In there. You better not disturb her, the way she feels."

Will had intended to ask if he could go to the scene of the trouble. Now he knew his duty was to stay and give what comfort he could to the womenfolk. He just hoped his father wouldn't get involved in the battle. At least he hadn't taken the long-barreled rifle with him. It still rested on the two wooden pegs above the fireplace.

More to occupy himself than for any other reason, Will took the heavy gun down and made sure it was loaded. Faith watched him fearfully.

"You—you aren't getting ready to shoot at anybody, are you?" she asked.

"No," he said. "Not unless the British come to attack us. But don't worry. They're a long way off."

Just then his mother came out of the bedroom and saw him. "Willing," she said, "put that instrument of death back where you found it."

There was a cold edge to her voice that allowed for no trifling. Without a word he replaced the rifle.

"Since we're not in any danger here," said his mother, "I see no reason why you shouldn't go back to your field work."

Four

Ezra Hand came home an hour before suppertime. Instead of going into the house, he turned toward the cornfield, and Will saw him striding along between the green rows.

"Well, son," he remarked with satisfaction, "we drove 'em off."

"You mean you were there, Dad?"

"I didn't take a hand, but I saw most of it. The lobsterbacks were headin' for their boats. Must ha' had a dozen or fifteen cows with 'em. They were right down at the water's edge when Springer's boys opened fire. Killed one cow an' knocked over a couple o' the British. But they got the rest o' the cattle aboard two boats an' started rowin'. It was about then that our boys brought up a cannon. Whoever aimed it did a good job, for they sank one o' the boats. It was quite a sight—the water full o' sailors an' cows, all thrashin' around together! The other boats picked up their men, but six o' the cattle got ashore. I reckon that'll discourage 'em some."

"Gosh, Dad!" Will exclaimed. "I wish I'd been there, too. Don't you think I'm old enough to join up with the militia now?"

Ezra Hand shook his head. "No," he said firmly. "Maybe I've got other plans for you. We'll wait an' see. Let's go back to the house. You've done a fair day's work."

Will's mother greeted them with curt disapproval. Though she was a staunch patriot, she didn't want her menfolk involved in the fighting if there was any way to avoid it.

By the time supper was on the table, most of her coolness had worn off, and she could hardly help listening with interest to her husband's account of the skirmish.

"Who was it lost the cattle?" she asked. "Anybody we know?"

"Yes," he told her, "the Widow Simpkins was one. They took her only milk cow an' a good heifer. Most of 'em were stolen from Jonas Stites's farm. I guess he can afford it, but the neighbors'll get together to help the widow."

While the girls were washing the dishes, Will and his father went out to the barn to do the milking.

"I don't much like the place we hid the sloop," Ezra Hand said with a frown. "Somebody sure cut that moorin' line. Besides, with the British comin' ashore to raid, they might just pick that cove to land in. Tide'll be high around dark. I think we'd better move her tonight."

"Good," said Will. "Where'll we take her?"

45

"Down to Town Creek, I guess. She'll be closer to the farm there, an' we can keep an eye on her."

They set off half an hour later, going on foot instead of riding. The sun went down when they were still half a mile from Cox Hall Creek, but there was some light left in the sky over Delaware Bay. From the top of the bluff, they took a long look westward.

"See anything out there?" the captain asked his son.

"I think so," Will replied. "Topsails, way out yonder. I'd say there were two British men-o'-war, about six or seven miles off."

His father nodded. "That's what I thought, too. Come on, we'll have no trouble from them."

If Hannibal was surprised to see them, he gave no sign of it. He got up from the hatch coaming, laid down his gun, and grinned in greeting.

In a few words the captain explained his plan, and the cook agreed. "I figgered you'd want to move her," he said. "Be a lot safer."

The tide was almost high, and there was plenty of water in the cove as Will cast off the moorings. Then he and Hannibal poled the vessel out of its place of concealment while his father steered. After they were clear of the mouth of the creek, the mainsail was quickly hoisted and the centerboard dropped. With a northerly breeze behind her, the *Fair Molly* slipped quietly down the bay shore.

Town Creek, or "New England Creek" as the old whalers had called it, was only about two miles to the south. They reached it in the early dusk and sailed into the narrow opening. There the centerboard was raised again,

46

and the polers went to work. The creek wound in and out among the marshes, but its channel was fairly deep. At last they reached a place where the shores were higher and a gnarled old cedar tree grew close to the bank.

"Tie her up," the skipper ordered. "The tree'll help hide the mast. You know where we are, Hannibal? The farm's right up yonder, less'n a mile away. If anything happens, you can come an' warn us."

The cook nodded. "Anybody come snoopin' 'round here," he replied, "is liable to find hisself full o' lead."

Will and his father set off through the tall reeds and were soon crossing the fields of a farm. After ten minutes they came out on the road only a few hundred yards from their own place.

"Handy enough," Ezra Hand said with a grin. "An' I reckon that Ferd Leech won't be able to find the sloop—if it was him that tried to set her adrift."

"What about takin' her out again?" Will asked. "Isn't there a chance we'll be goin' up to the city?"

"Not while the war goes on," his father told him. "Next time we take her out, it'll be a different kind o' voyage."

Will felt a surge of excitement at the words, but he knew better than to ask any more questions. There was a candle in the kitchen window. They let themselves in and tiptoed off to bed. But it took Will a while to get to sleep. In his imagination he saw himself, cutlass in hand, boarding a British ship. The only construction he could put on his father's hint was that the *Fair Molly* would soon become a privateer!

❖   ❖   ❖

Early the next morning Ezra Hand rode off in the heavy wagon without saying where he was going. Will's mother looked disapproving, but all she said was that Will had better finish his hoeing.

The breeze had died down, and it was hot once more in the field. As he toiled between the green rows of waist-high corn, he felt some envy of Hannibal, who was probably napping on the deck or fishing for crabs in the creek. As long as the sloop was so well hidden, Will saw no reason why the cook shouldn't be helping him.

It was late afternoon when his father came home. The mare looked tired, and lashed on the wagon bed was what appeared to be a heavy load, covered by a tarpaulin. It was hauled into the barn and left there while old Bess was unharnessed and put in her stall.

Ezra Hand saw his son staring at the odd-shaped load and spoke sharply. "You leave that canvas right where it is, Will," he said. "You'll find out in good time what's under it."

Will had no thought of disobeying his father's orders, but he stayed behind when the captain went into the house. After all, he thought, nothing had been said about not *touching* the tarpaulin. He ran a hand tentatively over the big hump in the middle and felt something long and rounded, like a smooth log. Only it didn't feel like wood. It was metal—iron, perhaps!

He closed the barn door and followed his father into the kitchen, his heart beating faster as he thought of what was in the wagon. Ezra Hand seemed preoccupied that evening. He said nothing at supper about where he had been all day, and Will's mother didn't attempt to ask him. After the chores were done, the two girls took their Saturday night baths in a large washtub in the kitchen. Will, being a boy, was allowed to bathe in a little fresh-water pond that lay in a wooded hollow below the farm. He took soap and a towel with him and undressed behind the bushes. In a moment he was splashing in the cool, shallow water, while a turtle looked on from a log and bullfrogs croaked in the reeds.

Well scrubbed and dried, Will returned to the house feeling refreshed. Dusk had fallen, and he knew his mother would worry if he didn't come in soon. But the mystery of what was concealed in the wagon was too strong to resist, and he tiptoed to the barn. As he approached the door, he could see light from a lantern shining through the cracks. Then he heard voices inside.

"We'll need a couple more men to handle her," his father was saying.

Another man, whose voice Will didn't recognize, answered. "I'll have 'em here tomorrow night," he said, "along with more powder an' a few more rounds o' shot. Ought to have the job all done before daylight."

There were sounds of movement, as if the two men were preparing to come out, and Will left in a hurry. He was undressed and getting into bed when he heard his father come in.

※　　　※　　　※

After breakfast on Sunday, the Hand family got ready to go to church. Hot and uncomfortable in his best clothes,

49

Will waited on the back steps for his parents and sisters to appear.

Usually, if the weather was at all bad, the wagon was used to take them to the Cold Spring Presbyterian Church, half a mile away. However, when the others came out, Will's father announced heartily that it was a fine day and everyone would walk.

"Then we'd better start," Martha Hand replied tartly. "Have to take it slow or we'll get sunstroke."

She and the girls wore wide-brimmed bonnets to protect their complexions, but though their white dresses looked cool enough, Will knew they concealed several layers of petticoats. He wondered how womenfolk could stand it.

The road was deep in dust. Once, when a neighbor's carryall passed, such clouds of dust arose that the Hands had to take to the high grass along the roadside. At last they reached the churchyard and went into the cool, dark interior. There Martha Hand sat very straight in their pew, vigorously wielding a palm-leaf fan. From the set of her chin, Will knew she had a low opinion of having to walk to church on a hot midsummer day.

The service, as usual, was a long one. The minister was in the middle of his sermon, having just come to "Fourthly," when the church windows rattled to the report of a gun. At once, half a dozen young men sprang from their seats and hurriedly tiptoed out.

After the stir in the congregation had subsided, the sermon droned on. Then came a new disturbance. Captain Isaac Smith, the coffinmaker, hurried down the aisle and plucked Ezra Hand's sleeve, whispering something in his ear. Instantly Will's father jumped up and followed the militia captain from the church.

The minister cut off his sermon in the middle of a sentence and called for the closing hymn. And three minutes later most of the people had hastened outside.

"It's the British!" young Joel Jenkins told Will. "They're offshore in their landin' boats, an' it looks like they're headin' for Cox Hall Creek. The militiamen have all gone home to get their guns."

"Where'd my dad go?" Will asked.

"I dunno. Somebody said he was bringin' a cannon."

Will stared at him, open-mouthed. A cannon! So he had been right about the thing hidden in the wagon! He didn't wait for his mother and sisters. Pulling off his jacket, he set out for home as fast as he could run.

As he cut across a field, he saw his father driving old Bess up the road at a gallop, with the same tarpaulin-covered cargo behind him in the wagon.

It took Will only a minute to change into old clothes, and while he dressed, he was thinking hard. Why would a raiding party be landing at such an unlikely spot as Cox Hall Creek? There were no farms close by and no fresh water. Only one reason seemed to fit their action. They must be after the *Fair Molly*, which had so recently been hidden there. That meant that some informer on shore must have told them, not knowing the sloop had been moved. It was one more black mark against Mr. Ferdinand Leech, he decided.

Five

Long before the Hand ladies reached home, Will had saddled Black Prince and set off across country for the scene of the impending raid. He was unarmed, for the only weapon in the house had been taken down from the wall—probably by his father.

The colt fairly flew over the fences and across the fields. By the time Will reached the bluff above the cove, he could see a line of men crouching behind the bushes with muskets ready. Most of them were in homespun, though one or two of their officers wore the blue and buff of the American army.

Will dismounted and tied Prince's rein to a tree. None of the militiamen paid any attention to him, but he noticed that the officers were looking south along the road, shielding their eyes from the sun. Then there came a clop of hoofs, and his father's wagon appeared. The old mare was lathered with sweat now and moved at a stumbling trot.

At once the soldiers sprang to their feet. A dozen of them ran to the wagon, stripped off the canvas, and began unloading the long-barreled nine-pounder that lay beneath it. Yet all the while they worked in silence. Will had to know why, so he made his way to the edge of the bluff and crawled through the brush on his belly till he had a view of the hidden anchorage where the *Fair Molly* had first put in.

Two miles or more offshore lay a huge British vessel—a seventy-four-gun ship-of-the-line, he was sure. And just entering the creek mouth were two longboats, each filled with sailors and marines. They rowed slowly and cautiously, with men in the bows checking the depth of the water by thrusting down poles. A smartly dressed young officer in the stern of the leading boat turned and hailed the craft behind him. He spoke in a low voice, but in the silence his words came plainly to the watchers above.

"There's no sloop here, sir," he said. "It must be our bird has flown."

"So it would seem," came the crisp reply. "I suggest, Mr. Thornhill, that you land your men anyway. Perhaps we can pick up a few more cattle. We'll wait here."

Will crept back out of the way, and a homespun-clad militiaman took his place. A whisper came along the line—"Hold your fire! Wait till they start climbin'."

There was a sound behind him, and when Will looked around, he saw the cannon being rolled up. But his attention was instantly drawn back to the line of riflemen.

A series of clicks told him they were cocking their weapons. Then an officer stood up with a yell.

"Let 'em have it!" he shouted, and the command was drowned out by the roar of gunfire. Below, on the path where the red-coated marines were climbing, there was instant confusion. Men who had been hit by that first volley fell backward into the arms of the men behind them. Some of the marines attempted to form a line and fire, but as fast as the Americans could load, they poured more bullets into them. Within less than a minute, the attacking force was tumbling pell-mell down the hill to the boat.

"Cease fire!" the Yankee captain ordered. "Let 'em get their wounded out!"

But the quiet didn't last long. The senior officer in the other boat was furious at the setback. He commanded his marines to stand and fire at the men on the bluff. The volley felled two Americans, and at once their angry comrades returned it.

The nine-pounder had been run up to the edge of the bluff and now Captain Isaac Smith took charge of aiming the piece. If it had been loaded with grape or canister, it might have killed a good many of the British force, but the only ammunition available was solid shot. When the slow match was applied to the touchhole, the cannon roared, and a heavy sphere of iron knocked a hole in the second boat's bottom.

There was no more fight left in the raiders. They scrambled for shore while the Yankee militiamen cheered derisively. A few seconds later, all that were left of the landing party were rowing madly toward the bay in the undamaged boat. It was a complete victory for the Americans.

"Hold on now!" called Lieutenant Joshua Townsend. "There's still a job to do. You, Jake, take some men down an' pick up the bodies. If there's any wounded, we'll try to take care of 'em."

Even though he wasn't in the militia, Will hurried to help. At the foot of the path, they found three of the enemy dead. And lying in the mud at the spot where the first boat had landed, Will came on the young British officer— a lad no older than himelf. He was bleeding heavily from a chest wound just above the heart, but he was still alive and gasping for breath.

"Hey!" Will called. "This one's wounded! Somebody give me a hand!"

With the help of two others, he carried the young officer to the top of the bluff and laid him on a piece of canvas. Captain Townsend came and knelt beside him, examining the wound.

"You got a horse here, Will?" he asked. "Ride up to Fishing Creek an' get Doc Leaming. Tell him to come to Amos Hughes's place. We'll carry the boy there. You better make it lively, though. This youngster's lost a lot o' blood."

Will was eager to help in any way he could. He jumped on the colt and galloped off northward by the same track he had used the week before. Going through the woods, he kept a careful watch. It was possible, he thought, that Ferd Leech was lurking there again, waiting to see the result of the raid. But this time there was no sign of him.

Luck was with Will, however, in the more pressing matter of locating the doctor. As he neared the village, he met a horseman plodding toward him and recognized the dark coat and bearded face of Dr. Leaming in person. It took him only a moment to deliver his message. The doctor spurred his horse to a trot, and Will turned the colt to accompany him.

In twenty minutes they reached the Hughes house, where a knot of militiamen stood talking in the yard.

"He's still alive," Aaron Ludlam told Will. "Sinkin' fast, though."

Meanwhile, the doctor had hurried inside, carrying his bag of instruments. It was half an hour before he reappeared. His face was grave, but he told the men he thought the young prisoner had an even chance to recover.

Looking around, Will saw his father's wagon, which had been used to carry the wounded youth. And a moment after, Ezra Hand came out of the house.

"Will," he said, "it's a good thing you brought the doctor so quick. He stopped the bleedin' an' took out the bullet. What the boy needs now is rest. But soon as he starts to get better, I want to take him down to our house an' let your ma feed him up with some o' her good cookin'. He seems like a nice young feller."

He climbed to the seat of the wagon and picked up the reins. "You ride on home," he told his son. "The womenfolks must be worried. Tell 'em I'm comin' right along, but the mare's too tired to move fast."

Will found his mother and sisters in the kitchen and told them in a few words what had happened since they left the church.

"A fine time for the British to come!" said Martha Hand.

"There'll be Sunday dinners spoiled all over this end o' the county! I'm not sure this roast'll be fit to eat!"

By Tuesday, with all the hoeing out of the way, Will invented an excuse to ride down to Cape Island. There had been fog at dawn, and it was still cool and cloudy when he hitched the colt to the rail behind the Atlantic Hotel. Very few guests were out, and none had ventured into the water.

However, when he sauntered down to the beach, he saw a single figure standing on the sand. It was Kate Perry. Her long skirts were blowing in the breeze, and she was watching the terns as they wheeled and screamed above the surf. When he came to stand beside her, she didn't seem surprised.

"I sort of expected you might be here, Will," she said with a laugh. "Or didn't you know this was our last day? We're taking the stage home tomorrow."

"Glad I came, then," he told her. "It's too bad we can't take you up in the *Fair Molly,* but I guess her packet days are over."

"I know," she said. "I'd much rather go with you than in that bumpy old coach. Is it true that the British tried to capture the sloop last Sunday?"

He told her about it, trying to make light of his own part in the affair. "Dad hasn't told me right out," he concluded, "but I'm sure he's goin' to put a cannon aboard the sloop, an' we'll sail her out as a privateer."

Kate's eyes were no longer mischievous. "That will be dangerous, won't it?" she said quietly. "She's such a little boat, and the warships look so big. I'll be worrying about you, Will."

They strolled along the beach in silence for a while. Then a bell was rung on the hotel porch—the call to the midday dinner.

"I'm afraid I have to go," said Kate sadly. "I hope you'll write to me, Will. I'll be watching the papers for news."

She gave him both her hands in farewell, then smiled and left him, running up the dune. Will watched her till she was in the building. Riding home, he didn't know whether to be happy or sad.

❖   ❖   ❖

"We'll mount the gun forward o' the mast," Ezra Hand told the five young men who had come to help arm the *Fair Molly*. "The shot locker can go right here by the foot o' the mast, an' we'll store the powder below decks. You, Will, an' Hannibal, give these boys a hand."

The cannon had already been unloaded from the wagon. Now it lay on the creek bank. The only way to get it aboard the sloop was to carry it over the makeshift gangplank—two wide boards laid across the intervening water.

They put stout ropes under either end of the gun. Then Hannibal and the strongest of the young men lifted the heavier end—the breach—while two more picked up the muzzle. The boards bent alarmingly under their weight, and they had to inch across, moving one short step at a time. Once it was across the sloop's gunwale, Will was able to lend a hand.

The carriage was a low frame of heavy oak timbers, mounted on small iron wheels in the usual naval fashion. When it was in place, they lifted the gun and fitted the round trunnions on either side into the greased sockets of the carriage. Ropes attached to the four corners made it possible to swing the cannon so as to point forward or to either side. And a long iron screw could lift or lower the muzzle.

Will stood back to admire the formidable weapon. The only question in his mind was who would have charge of loading and firing the cannon. He knew his father had no special skill in gunnery.

"All right, lads," the captain told his helpers, "come up to the house an' we'll see if the ladies have some refreshments ready. I don't have to tell you to keep quiet about where you've been today. There's reason to think there are traitors nearby who'd dearly love to do the sloop harm if they knew where to find her."

"Dad," said Will as they walked homeward, "how are you goin' to get a man to be your gunner?"

His father chuckled. "Had him all lined up 'fore I got the cannon. Somebody you know right well, but I reckon you'd never guess. It's Hannibal. He isn't one to brag, but he was a gunner's mate under Decatur on the *Enterprise* when they sailed into Tripoli against the pirates in 1804. There are a few others I've picked to go as crew."

"How about me?" asked Will eagerly.

"Well," the captain replied, "if we can persuade your ma to let you go, I'd sort o' counted on it. Don't get to thinkin' it'll be any picnic, though. It's rough, hard work, an' dangerous."

Will was jubilant. Being a sailor on a privateer, he thought, was a lot better than hoeing or marching with the militia.

When the party reached the house, they were greeted by Faith and Lovey, who brought out pitchers of sweet raspberry juice, sometimes called "shrub," and plates heaped high with cookies. The youths vowed they would gladly work twice as hard for such a reward, and the two girls giggled with pleasure.

The next morning Ezra Hand rode off to the county seat at Middle Town, saying merely that he had important business there. But when he returned, late in the afternoon, Will could see he was pleased about something. After supper he produced an official-looking paper.

"Here y'are, Will," he said. "It's our letter o' marque, all signed an' sealed. Now we're ready to go privateerin', just as soon as we can get the sloop in shape!"

The sailing didn't take place quite as quickly as Will would have liked. Powder was easily obtained, but it took time to procure the canister, chain shot, and solid ball that were needed for the gun. Meanwhile, Martha Hand made some difficulties over having her boy sail in the crew.

"He's too young," she insisted. "And he's the only son we'll ever have."

The captain knew better than to argue. He merely winked at Will and assured him privately that his mother would "come 'round."

At the end of July, word came that the ammunition was ready, and Ezra Hand set off in the wagon for Fishing Creek, where the artillery company was holding it for him. He told his son to go down to the sloop and tell Hannibal it was coming.

Will hiked over through the meadows to the marsh, listening to the trilling of red-winged blackbirds and the harsh laughter of gulls. Not far from the sloop's hiding place, the path led through a jungle of ten-foot bulrushes.

Suddenly there was a startled grunt right in front of him, followed by a sound of running feet and a crashing among the canelike stems of the reeds.

Without an instant's delay, Will dashed after the man or animal that had made the noise. The trail of broken bulrushes wasn't hard to follow, but after a few moments he found himself in a bog, where the water was up to his knees. He waded back to the bank and stood listening. There were no more sounds, but in the mud he saw a footprint—the fresh track of a man's boot, heading away from the creek.

Someone—and he thought he knew who—had discovered the location of the *Fair Molly*.

Six

Will tried to follow the tracks of the interloper, but after a few minutes he realized it was hopeless. He found no more footprints, and when he came to a patch of woods, there were no more broken reeds to show where the man had gone. Out of breath and disgusted, he returned to the creek bank and eventually reached the sloop.

"What you been chasin'?" Hannibal asked. "Thought I heard somebody runnin'."

When he heard Will's story, he shook his head. "Bad business to stay here much longer," he commented. "You say yo' paw's bringin' the shot?"

"That's right. I figure he'll be ready to sail by tomorrow."

"Hmm," grunted Hannibal. "Could be that ain't quick enough. You better run home an' tell him what's happenin'."

Captain Hand got back to the farm by noon, once more bringing a heavy load covered by a tarpaulin. When Will told him of his experience that morning, his father looked grave.

"Hannibal's right," he said. "We'd better move the sloop tonight. I reckon the best plan would be to sail her clear 'round the point an' tie up in Cold Spring Inlet."

"You want to put the cannon shot aboard first?" Will asked.

"No. Time enough for that after we're sure she's safe. We'll want less weight tonight anyhow if we're to get in over the bar."

At sunset they walked together down to the sloop's mooring and found Hannibal standing guard.

"When's high tide?" the captain asked.

"Jus' turned—'bout half an hour ago," the cook told him.

They made their preparations to raise the mainsail and run up the jib. "Let's hope," said Ezra Hand, "there's no enemy ship outside, waitin' for us. If that feller Will heard has sent word to the British, we may get caught. We'll just have to chance it."

So it was with a scared and excited feeling that Will cast off the moorings as dusk came on. A light southerly breeze filled the sails, and the *Fair Molly* crept down the winding creek while Hannibal fended off the bank with an oar. It was almost dark when they reached the narrow mouth.

"Will," his father ordered, "skip up to the masthead an' see if there's anything in sight."

Scrambling aloft, he had a clear view of the bay. A

couple of miles off, he saw the riding lights of a ship, but there seemed to be no sign of any smaller craft nearer shore. He took enough time to be certain, then slid down a rope and reported to the captain.

"Here we go, then," Ezra Hand grunted. "Get ready to drop the centerboard soon as we're outside."

Shortly they were in the deep water of the bay and tacking southward to clear Cape May Point. The lighthouse, built there several years earlier, was dark, for the men of the county thought it might aid the British. Knowing the coast as he did, Ezra Hand needed no beacon to give him his bearings.

About ten that night, the sloop had made her eastward reach and was off the broad mouth of Cold Spring Inlet. It was almost pitch dark. No lights shone in the windows on Cape Island, for most of the local residents went early to bed. But the skipper steered in through the channel that crossed the bar, followed the windings of the inlet, and brought the sloop smartly about. In a moment she had drifted in alongside the barnacle-covered piling of a fisherman's dock. Quickly the sails were snugged down, and the *Fair Molly* was safely moored.

"This," Ezra Hand told Hannibal, "is Lem Schellenger's dock. I know he won't mind our tyin' up here, an' you should be safe enough from the British. The militia's got gun emplacements both sides o' the inlet."

He and Will bade the cook good night and started back to the farm. The distance was considerably farther than from Town Creek, but they reached home well before midnight.

Will slept well, his mind clear of worries about the

sloop's safety. Even if a spy had seen them take her around the point, there was little that could be done to harm her in such a well-defended spot.

At breakfast the next morning, his father announced that he was going to get the wounded prisoner at Amos Hughes's farm. "They tell me he's enough better so he can be moved," he said. "An' Lieutenant Townsend has his parole that he won't try to escape."

Martha Hand was doubtful but agreed to go with her husband and take a look at the young man.

When they had ridden off, Faithful told Will how her mother felt about enemy prisoners.

"She thinks they're dangerous critters." The girl chuckled. "I wouldn't be surprised if she looks for horns and a tail!"

"He seemed to me to be a nice enough young man," said Will. "Really just a boy, he was, an' hurt so bad that he couldn't hurt a fly. I bet Ma'll get to like him. His name's Roger Thornhill."

Will was there in the dooryard when his parents returned. The prisoner lay on a straw mattress in the wagon body. His face was drawn and white.

"I reckon the joltin' tired him out," said Will's father. "Give me a hand, an' we'll carry him in."

Will wasn't too surprised to see his mother hurrying ahead to prepare a bed in the front parlor. She acted as concerned as if the youth had been her own son. They made him as comfortable as they could, sponged his face with cold water, and gave him a glass of milk. Then they tiptoed out to let him rest.

Late that afternoon, when young Thornhill had slept and seemed to feel better, Will and the girls had a chat with him. He was only sixteen, they learned. Two years earlier he had joined the Royal Navy as a midshipman, and he had been in command of the leading boat when they rowed into Cox Hall Creek.

"The captain had word from shore," he explained, "that a Yankee vessel was hidden there, and we were sent in to take her. I stayed with the boat, as an officer should, and was hit by your first volley. After that I don't remember anything till the doctor was working on me."

"Where's your home?" Lovey asked.

"It's in flat farming country, not very different from this," he said. "Our village is in Suffolk, a few miles from Harwich Port. My father's a clergyman."

"I don't suppose," Will put in, "that you'd know how your captain found out about the sloop?"

Roger smiled. "The soldiers asked me that. I'm not sure, but I think someone signaled with a light from the shore. I only wish he had told of the trap we were going into."

There was no malice in his words. He seemed to take his predicament calmly, as one of the fortunes of war. The two girls were fascinated by his educated British accent. And though he was pale and thin, there was no denying his good looks. He had fine features, and a mop of blond curls hung over his forehead. There was no question, Will thought, that he would have plenty of nursing in that household.

Martha Hand was almost as much captivated as her daughters. She cooked special dishes to tempt his appetite and changed his bandages with professional care.

The captain shared Will's amusement in these developments. "Your ma sure had a change o' heart," he said. "Maybe a good thing, too. It'll help take her mind off the *Fair Molly* when we put to sea."

"When will that be?" his son asked eagerly.

"Just a day or two, I reckon. The ammunition's already aboard, an' we'll stock the sloop with food tomorrow. Then the crew's promised to come aboard the next day. I wouldn't say anything about it to Roger or the girls. I trust him to keep his parole, but no need to tempt him other ways."

In the morning Will helped his father fill the wagon with sacks of potatoes, a side of bacon, bags of cornmeal and flour, and a barrel of apples. Finally the skipper carefully carried a crate of eggs to stow on top.

"Hannibal's got all the salt an' sugar an' coffee we need," he said. "An' in slack times the boys'll catch some fish. We ought to eat well enough."

As they drove down the road to Cape Island, they had to pull out to let the northbound stage pass. It gave Will a twinge of melancholy to think that Kate Perry had been in the same coach a few days before. He remembered he had promised that he would write to her. Well, there'd be time for that after the first privateering voyage, when he hoped there might be something really interesting to tell her.

At the wharf in Cold Spring Harbor they found Hannibal and the *Fair Molly* safe and sound. One of the crew was there, too. It was Aaron Schellenger, a strapping young fisherman, a year older than Will. He helped them carry the provisions below. Then Will drove the wagon home and stabled the mare. It was midafternoon when he got back to the sloop.

The cabin, formerly used by packet passengers, had some new berths, built by Hannibal in leisure time, and there the crew would be quartered. Soon more men began to arrive. Matthew Hughes, of Cape Island, and Jonathan Jenkins, of Green Creek, were both friends of Will's. They had been around boats most of their lives and also knew how to handle firearms. The last to arrive was Amos Stilwell, the mate. Like Captain Hand he had a pilot's certificate and was not only a good navigator but also an older man, used to command.

They chose their bunks and stowed their gear with a little good-natured horseplay. Several children and two or three elderly men had gathered at the dock, drawn by curiosity. At first Will was uneasy about this, but he realized it would be impossible to keep the sloop's movements secret in such a public place. All he could do was hope the mysterious spy wouldn't be told about them.

The audience on the dock must have annoyed Will's father, too, for he ordered the men to cast off and hoist the mainsail. Sailing out into the middle of the inlet, he hove to and called the hands aft.

"No point in tellin' the whole town our plans," he said. "When we sail out tonight, I'd like to head back around the cape. From there we'll cruise up along the shore. Somebody's been sendin' signals to the British fleet, an' I'd like to find out how they do it. So I'll want a sharp lookout at the masthead, watchin' for lights.

"This ought to be a good night for it. No moon an' a

calm sea. We'll lie here a spell an' won't go out till it's good an' dark."

Hannibal cooked them their first supper aboard, and they sat on the forehatch talking until after sundown. Amos Stilwell puffed contentedly at a smelly old pipe while he and the captain discussed the coming voyage in hushed voices. About ten o'clock Will's father called all hands and made ready to sail out.

In spite of the darkness, he steered through the narrow inlet and out over the bar without trouble. Will had been given the first watch aloft, and as soon as they were outside, he searched the horizon with care. There was no sail in sight. A long swell rocked the hull, and his perch swayed slowly from side to side. He was too good a sailor to be seasick.

The *Fair Molly* had rounded Cape May Point and was off Pond Creek before Will saw anything interesting. Then he made out a big ship off to port. She was well over a mile away and apparently at anchor, for she carried only a small riding sail at her mizzen. There were no lights showing along her side.

In a low voice he hailed the deck. "Ship off the port bow," he told the skipper. "Seems to be anchored."

"How far is she?" his father asked.

"Mile an' a half, I'd guess. No riding lights."

"All right. Keep an eye on her."

They sailed on in silence up the shore. Past Town Creek —past Cox Hall Creek—and on beneath the high bluffs south of Fishing Creek. Will thought it must be nearly midnight, and his arms and legs were getting cramped from his

uncomfortable position at the masthead when he saw a
light blinking. It was on the top of the bluff in the woods.
He was sure there was no house near the spot. The light
appeared and disappeared in irregular flashes, some long,
some short.

"Look, Dad!" he whispered down hoarsely. "On the bluff!"

For a moment his father didn't answer. Then he told Will to look out into the bay. "See anything there?" he asked in the same low voice.

"Yes! There's a ship out in the main channel, an' she's flashin' lights, too!"

The men on deck stirred in excitement, but they kept quiet, too. The sloop swung in closer to the shore so that the signal light was hidden even from Will's eyes. He realized that his father didn't want the little vessel to be seen from up there on the bluff. Without being told, he slid down to the deck and stood ready to help.

In spite of the darkness, he knew they were now very close to the mouth of Fishing Creek, and it was no surprise to him when his father swung the tiller over and slacked the sheet. The sloop turned neatly into the entrance. Will hauled up the centerboard, and they drifted silently in along the south bank.

"Good enough," the captain muttered. "We'll hold her here. Amos, you take two men with guns an' see if you can catch that sneakin' spy up there. Will, you saw where he was. Go along an' show 'em."

It took a moment to pick up the muskets, check their priming, and go over the side. Then they were climbing the steep bank. Will's heart beat fast as he led the way along the bluff top into the woods. It was country he knew well. Even in the dark he could move fairly fast, and he was careful not to step on any dead branches. Matt Hughes, behind him, was less skillful. There was a crash and a smothered exclamation as he fell over a root.

"Sh! Quiet, there!" the mate warned in a whisper. Will halted, listening. Suddenly, a little way ahead of him, he heard another twig snap.

"Come on!" he urged. "The man's gettin' away!"

They went stumbling toward the sound at the best speed they could manage. The crackling noise of the man's flight was now plain for all to hear. He must have given up any attempt to be quiet and was running for his life.

"Halt!" shouted Amos Stilwell. "Halt or we'll shoot!"

But the only effect was a faster drumming of feet as the fleeing man pulled away from his pursuers. After two or three minutes of blind running, Stilwell stopped them.

"No use," he panted. "Feller knows the woods better'n we do. One of us is likely to bash himself against a tree."

"I reckon I could find him," Will said. "My guess is he'll head straight for Leech's Tavern. I've seen Ferd Leech skulkin' around here before."

"No proof unless we caught him red-handed," the mate told him. "Let's head toward the shore an' see if we can find some evidence—locate the spot where he was flashin' the light."

Reluctantly they turned westward and approached the edge of the bluff. Soon they came to a little clearing, but it was too dark to look for clues. "Here," said Stilwell. "Fetch me a pitch-pine branch. We'll have to make us a torch!"

Seven

Young Schellenger jerked a low limb from a pine tree, and it was fairly dripping with sap that had an odor like turpentine. In a moment the mate had struck fire with flint and steel. The torch blazed up, lighting the cleared space, and while Matt Hughes stood guard, the others began their search.

About ten feet back from the edge of the bluff, Will found a flat stump. He sniffed at it and called the mate.

"Smell that," he said. "Whale oil, isn't it?"

"Sure 'nough," Amos Stilwell agreed. "He set his lantern here on the stump! An' there's a clear view from here way out into the bay."

Will stared off across the water. He could barely make out the outline of a ship—a frigate or corvette, he thought —but there was no light flashing from her deck. The torch, he knew, must be visible to her crew, and he wondered what they might be thinking of its erratic motion.

"Well, boys," said the mate, "our spy's got away. 'Bout all we can do now is get back to the sloop."

It hurt Will's pride to have nothing better to report, but at least they were sure of the spot used for signaling. Captain Hand heard what they had to tell in silence.

"All right," he said at length, "let's make sail an' get out o' here. I'll send word to Josh Townsend about it tomor·row."

The *Fair Molly* cleared the creek mouth and headed north again till she was off the entrance to Green Creek. There the skipper put her about.

"Less'n three hours left till daylight," he said. "An' unless the wind shifts, we'll have to tack most o' the way home."

"Gee, Dad," Will expostulated. "I thought we were goin' to stay out till we captured a prize!"

"You let me do the thinkin'," Ezra Hand replied sharply. "Go forward an' up to the masthead an' keep your eyes peeled."

From his high perch, the stars seemed brighter than ever, and his vision was sharper. Time passed, and they were down within sight of the larger ship once more. She was still in the same position, but as Will's eyes scanned the horizon ahead, he was startled to see a smaller dark object moving toward the shore. It was about a half mile south of them and going at a good clip.

"Boat dead ahead!" Will called to the deck. "She's headed for Pond Creek."

"Hannibal," he heard his father order, "you better get

75

your bow gun loaded an' ready. I reckon that's a British longboat, goin' ashore for water. The rest o' you boys, prime your muskets."

In his excitement Will nearly fell out of the crosstrees. It was difficult to keep his teeth from chattering, not because he was scared but because the predawn breeze blew chilly from the west. Close-hauled, the *Fair Molly* was making better speed on her southward course.

It was hard to tell whether anyone in the longboat had observed the sloop as yet. At any rate, the rowers were sending her rapidly toward shore, and she would be in Pond Creek long before they could close with her.

"Come on down, Will," he heard his father call. The skipper brought the sloop's head into the wind and held her there with sails flapping. "We'll wait an' see what happens," he said. "Aaron, that's near your place. Any militia quartered around there?"

"No, sir," Schellenger answered. "But I think they're camped a mile or so back in the woods. The folks down here do keep a watch, an' maybe somebody sent for help."

The sloop stood off the creek entrance for close to a quarter of an hour, all hands listening. Possibly all the British wanted was fresh water, but if they were after meat, some farmer might start shooting.

Suddenly the silence was broken by a rattle of musket fire. They heard distant yelling, too, and then more scattered shots.

"Here we go," said the captain. "Man your gun, boys."

He brought the sloop over before the wind and sent her charging in toward the creek mouth. Forward, Hannibal had rammed home a charge of grapeshot on top of the powder bag.

"Grab hold o' those ropes," he told Will and Jonathan Jenkins. "Get ready to haul the gun 'round when I tell you."

A hundred yards from shore, Ezra Hand turned into the wind again. "Got to have a little sea room," he explained. "Too close in, we might get blown on shore. I reckon they'll be comin' out pretty quick."

The breeze had strengthened and was drifting them shoreward faster than they had realized. Suddenly Will felt the sloop lurch as her centerboard struck a sandbank, and before it could be raised, the deck was canted over at an angle. Frantically he and his father struggled to free the heavy plank and pull it up into its housing. But just as they felt it loosening from the shoal, Aaron Schellenger warned them that the longboat was coming out of the creek.

"Help Will haul this cussed thing up," snapped the captain. "I've got to take the helm."

By the time the centerboard was lifted, the ship's boat was right abreast of them, and they heard an officer shouting an order to the rowers.

"They're aimin' to board us!" the skipper told his crew. "Train your gun, Hannibal!"

Under the cook's quick commands, Will and Jonathan pulled inexpertly on the ropes. They had barely brought the muzzle to bear when the longboat's sailors shipped oars, ready to board.

Calmly Hannibal laid a lighted slow match to the

breach of the cannon, and the deck heaved to the recoil of the explosion.

Thrown to his knees, Will hung on to the rope and stared through the smoke. In the darkness and confusion, it was hard to see what had happened, but he heard screams of pain and then a choking voice ordering the rowers to give way.

When the smoke blew clear, he realized it was all over. Oars creaked in the tholepins as the boat drew hurriedly away, a dark shape against the paler gray of the water.

"Come on, boys," said Ezra Hand crisply. "We've got to move lively before they get back to their ship, or she'll blow us to kingdom come!"

They dropped the centerboard again and made all speed southward to Cape May Point. Hannibal swabbed out his gun, then came aft to report to the captain.

"Things was happenin' too quick," he said apologetically, "or I might have sunk 'em. I knew 'twas aimed too high. But that grapeshot must ha' done damage to anybody that was standin' up."

"You did fine," Captain Hand told him. "If we'd sunk their boat, we'd ha' been obliged to stand by an' pull 'em out o' the water. This way we drove 'em off, which is a lot better. How 'bout fixin' us some coffee? I reckon all hands could use a drink of it after that."

The gray of dawn was lightening the sky as the sloop bore off to round the point. Once more Will had climbed the mast to keep watch astern, and as his father expected, there was furious activity aboard the big British warship. With incredible speed her sails were unfurled—courses, topsails, topgallants—and she was filling away before the wind.

Every few moments Will hailed the deck to report what was happening. With all her canvas spread, the great ship was able to make far more speed than the *Fair Molly*, and now she was less than two miles astern. At that rate, she would be within long cannon-range before they were past Cape Island.

In the slant morning sunlight, Will could see a lot of excitement among the people along the beach. Some were running hither and thither, others waving at the privateer. If the sloop was to be blown out of the water, at least there would be plenty of witnesses.

In sight ahead, now, was the entrance to Cold Spring Inlet. And to Will's great joy he saw an American flag being run up at the gun emplacement on the nearer side. He hoped that meant some militiamen were there to man the big cannon.

Astern, there was a sudden puff of smoke from the Britisher's bow, and five or six seconds later he heard the heavy boom of a gun. The cannonball fell into the sea a hundred yards off, and a great spout of white water went up.

"Ready to come about!" the captain yelled. "We're goin' to beat 'em in this race yet!"

He swung the helm over as the main sheet was hauled in. The *Fair Molly* scudded over the bar and was behind the sheltering dune before another shot could be fired.

Eight

At the dock in Cold Spring Harbor, the sloop's arrival was hailed by a small crowd of excited people. Besides the native fishermen, Will saw several men whose city dress showed they were hotel guests, thrilled by a firsthand view of the war.

The tall ship-of-the-line was still cruising off the inlet, and her guns roared occasionally as she fired on the American defenses. Most of the shots plowed harmlessly into the sand. The Cape May men in the little fort held their fire, saving powder for a time when the need might be greater. They knew the British ship drew far too much water to come any nearer, and the only real danger was that she might send in boats.

Among the onlookers was an old Revolutionary War soldier named Abijah Reeves. "How's the privateerin', Ezra?" he asked Captain Hand with a wink. "Didn't capture any enemy vessels, did ye?"

"Not this time," the skipper replied. "Best we could do was tangle with that seventy-four-gunner out yonder." The old man cackled. "Yeh—I seen it. That's the *Poictiers*, with Commodore Beresford hisself in command. Reckon you was a mite outgunned!"

Ezra Hand drew Will aside. "I aim to stay here with the sloop," he said. "But we ought to get word to Josh Townsend about that signalin' business. I want you to go home an' get the colt. Ride to Middle Town, or wherever you can find him, an' tell him what you found. Then come back here. We may want to sail tonight."

Will reached the farm half an hour later and found his mother in the dooryard, scattering corn for the chickens. She looked up in delighted surprise.

"Why, Willing!" she exclaimed. "We thought o' course you were somewhere at sea!"

"Got chased into Cold Spring Inlet by a big ship," he told her sheepishly. "You got any breakfast left, Ma? I'm starved."

While she fried some eggs and poured him a big mug of milk, Will gave her a few details of their brief cruise. "We can't get out again till the ship's gone," he said. "But while we're waitin', Dad wants me to take a message to Josh Townsend. How's your patient?"

"He's better every day," she answered proudly. "Eats better an' gets plenty o' sleep. His wound'll be healed up in another two weeks, at this rate."

Will finished his breakfast and saddled Black Prince. He rode north half a mile and stopped at the Ludlam house to ask where Lieutenant Townsend was likely to be.

"The brigade's been movin' around a lot," Reuben Ludlam replied. "Last night I heard they drove off a boatload o' British at Pond Creek. If I was you, I'd look for 'em in the camp they've got, in the woods back o' Town Bank. An' if you see my boy, tell him he's needed to harvest the oats, soon as Josh can let him off."

Will promised to deliver the message and rode westward on a little side road, leading toward Town Bank. It was a fine August morning, with birds chirping in the bushes and the shrill call of katydids coming across the fields. He whistled as he rode.

Ahead of him he saw a small farmhouse, really a log cabin, backed up against the woods. He didn't know who lived there, but he rode up to the door, still whistling, and asked if anybody was at home. The words were hardly out of his mouth when a gruff voice came from the edge of the woods.

"Halt! Put up your hands an' get off that horse!"

Hesitantly he lifted his arms and looked to his left, where the voice had come from. A young militiaman had stepped from behind a tree and stood there pointing a musket at Will's head.

"Aw, shucks, Abel!" said Will with a laugh. "You know me well enough. I've got a message for Josh Townsend, if you can locate him."

His cousin, Abel Hand, lowered the gun and grinned. "All I saw was a hostile-lookin' feller ridin' a fancy black horse," he said. "We're tryin' to keep it a secret where we bivouac, so we take turns standin' guard. You better leave the colt with me an' go on into the woods afoot. Reckon you'll find the lieutenant all right."

There was a bare trace of a path leading into the thick forest, and Will went in with more caution after being challenged. Within a few hundred feet, he approached a small clearing and saw men standing or resting there. Fortunately the first one who looked up recognized him. It was Jesse Springer.

"Hi, there, Will," he said in a low voice. "What brings you here?"

"Something Dad wants me to tell Josh Townsend. Is he busy right now?"

"Reckon not. I'll take you over there."

Lieutenant Townsend was sitting on a stump, studying a map of Cape May County. But when Will began to tell his story, he gave him his full attention.

"Show me where you saw the light, here on the map," he said.

"Right about here," Will told him. "Maybe two miles north o' Cox Hall Creek an' only a few hundred yards below Fishin' Creek. It was close to the edge o' the bluff. Dad thinks if we hadn't kept movin' the sloop from one moorin' to another, the spy would have tipped the British off an' they'd have captured her."

Townsend nodded. "Seems so," he said. "How'd you folks make out last night? We were lucky to be ready for that boat when it came in, an' they left after one volley. But we saw your sail outside an' heard a cannon shot."

"That's right," Will told him. "They started to board us, but Hannibal fired the nine-pounder, an' the load o' grape-shot must have hit a few. Anyhow, they pulled away in a hurry an' went back to their ship. She pretty near caught us before we could get into Cold Spring Inlet."

"Glad you made it," said the officer. "How's that wounded prisoner getting along?"

"I didn't see him today, but Ma says he's doin' fine. Everybody likes him at our house. By the way, Reuben Ludlam says to tell you he needs his son home."

The lieutenant laughed. "Half the farmers in the county feel that way. We'll send a couple o' men to keep an eye on that signal station. I don't know whether your father wants my advice, but I hope he'll be extra careful when he sails out. Beresford's no fool, and he may be laying a trap for the *Fair Molly* right now."

Will thought over that warning as he rode homeward. If the big seventy-four still lay outside the inlet, of course his father wouldn't attempt to leave. But since she was flagship of the blockading fleet, he thought the commodore must have taken her back into Delaware Bay. Just to make sure, he turned the colt westward again and soon reached the bluff below Town Bank. One look showed him the *Poictiers* was on station once more, with two smaller warships cruising on either side.

Satisfied, he headed back to the farm. Noon was approaching, and he was hungry once more. There was no point in returning to the sloop for a few hours, since he was sure she couldn't sail in daylight. After stabling Black Prince, he went into the kitchen and found his mother busy making bread. Seated at the table was Roger Thornhill.

"Glad to see you up," said Will. "Feelin' better?"

"Aye," the young midshipman replied. "I've had the

best of nursing and such food as I've never tasted aboard ship—or even ashore, for that matter."

"Wash up, Will," said his mother. "We'll be sitting down to eat soon as the girls set the table."

He scrubbed his face and hands at the sink, filling a basin from the bucket of well water that sat there.

"What's a midshipman's job aboard a ship of war?" he asked the youthful prisoner.

Roger grinned. "At the first," he said, "he's no more than a ship's boy, trying to learn the ropes and steer clear of the bosun's cane. Then after two years or so of schooling in navigation and seamanship, he's made a sort of junior officer. We have our own quarters, a bit better than the forecastle, and we're given small commands, such as a gig or even a longboat. That boarding party," he added ruefully, "was my first real command. And now I'm out of the war!"

"Too bad!" Will sympathized. "But maybe by the time it's over, you'll want to give up the Royal Navy an' settle down around here."

"No," said Roger. "That would make me a deserter! Perhaps there will be an exchange of prisoners, and I can get back to my ship."

Faithful and Loving, putting plates and pewter on the table, were listening to this conversation with the greatest interest.

"Try not to get captured, Will!" said Faith. "We'd rather keep Roger here and not have him exchanged!"

Will shot her a warning glance, and she said nothing more. It was all very well, he thought, to like this English boy, but it would hardly be prudent to let him know about their privateering.

✿   ✿   ✿

About five that afternoon, Will left the farm and started back to Cold Spring Inlet. He knew the stock would be all right, for both the girls were used to doing the milking and feeding the pigs and cattle when the menfolk were away.

There seemed to be little activity around the dock where the *Fair Molly* was tied up. Hannibal sat on the forehatch cleaning fish, and Aaron Schellenger was netting crabs over the rail. Apparently the onlookers had had enough of this peaceful scene and gone back about their business.

"Where's Dad?" Will asked the cook.

Hannibal rolled his eyes toward the cabin. "Makin' plans with Mr. Stilwell," he replied in a low voice. "Don't do nothin' to make folks suspect we're goin' out again."

Will yawned and stretched deliberately, then joined Aaron, aft by the taffrail. "How are they bitin'?" he asked.

Aaron jiggled his line, baited with pork rind, and pointed to the bucket at his side. It was half filled with squirming crabs. Just then a big one grabbed at the bait with its claws, and Will took it in the net as Aaron pulled it out of water.

"You get word to Townsend about those signal lights?" he asked Will.

"Yep. If they try to signal from the same place, the militia'll nail 'em." Will lowered his voice. "You think anybody's watchin' us here?" he asked.

"I've kept an eye on the dock an' haven't seen anything suspicious. But o' course the sloop could be spotted easy enough from any place back amongst the houses."

By six o'clock Hannibal ladled out fish chowder for those present and started shelling the crabs Aaron had caught. Then the captain called Will into the cabin. When he had heard the boy's report, he nodded approvingly.

"You say you got a good look at the *Poictiers* back in the bay. I hope she stays there, for we're not doin' a whole lot for the country lyin' here. Soon as it's full dark, I reckon we'll try to get outside. I've picked a good, sharp boy— one o' Schellenger's young brothers—to wait out at the mouth o' the inlet an' watch for enemy sail."

The darkness seemed to come very slowly, but at last night had settled over Cape Island. One by one the other members of the crew appeared. Will and Matt Hughes moved silently to the mooring ropes and cast off when they were given the signal. Jenkins and Schellenger hauled up the mainsail, and the mate stood by at the jib halyards. In a moment the *Fair Molly* was gliding out through the winding inlet.

They were only twenty yards from the gun emplacement on the south bank when a small, dark figure appeared on the sandy dune. Its right arm went up, and Captain Hand grunted approval.

"Means there's nothing in sight," he told Will. "Go forrard an' help Mr. Stilwell get the topsail up soon as we're over the bar."

There was a freshening southeast wind, and the moment they were outside, the sloop heeled over on a reach to the northeast, along the coast. This present course would take them into less familiar waters but might offer better hunting.

Just as Will was relaxing after the strain of the last few minutes, he heard the smashing report of a cannon astern and nearly jumped out of his skin.

"That came from the fort!" said Aaron. "Wonder what they're firin' at!"

From his place at the helm, Ezra Hand barked an order. "Up to the masthead, Will! Tell me if you sight a sail."

He went aloft like a scared cat and clung there looking out astern. At first he could make out nothing in the darkness. Then he saw the dim line where the sea met the sky. Searching along it, his eyes stopped at a tiny blotch that broke the line of the horizon. Finally he was sure. A ship, schooner-rigged, he thought, was coming up fast from the southwest. As nearly as he could judge, the following vessel was still about two miles astern of them.

He hailed the deck and gave this information to his father, who didn't seem too surprised at the news. "Stay up there," he told Will. "Let me know if they start to gain on us much."

From his high perch, swaying to the push of the wind, it seemed to Will that the *Fair Molly* was fairly racing through the seas. Yet each time he looked aft, the pursuing schooner loomed a little larger.

"Ahoy, the deck!" he called at last. "She's gained, all right. Not much more'n a mile astern now. Pretty close to long gun-range!"

His father didn't answer him directly, but he heard the

order to let the sloop fall off to port, then to raise the centerboard. Staring westward, Will realized they were passing the upper end of Five Mile Beach. Ahead, as the bow swung shoreward, was the treacherous bar at Hereford Inlet.

"All right, boys," the skipper said calmly. "Steady as she goes. We'll be inside in a minute."

There was a white line of surf that seemed to run the full length of the bar, but Ezra Hand knew where the channel lay. Up to the last few seconds the gap was invisible. Then they were in it and through to the calmer water beyond. When Will returned to the deck at his father's order, he found the crew chuckling over the maneuver.

"She prob'ly draws five feet more water'n we do," said Aaron Schellenger. "So we don't need to worry about her followin' us in."

"That's right," Jonathan Jenkins agreed. "An' before she can train a gun, we'll be hid by those woods up yonder."

The privateer was, in fact, sailing comfortably up Great Channel with a beam wind and the forested dunes of Seven Mile Beach off to starboard. The tall trees that would conceal her were only half a mile away when Hannibal's sharp ears caught a sound.

"Hark!" he said suddenly and held up a warning hand. Then Will heard it—a faint grinding, crunching noise and then a far-off yell of terror.

"Bring her about!" roared the skipper, and swung the tiller as the crew manned the main sheet. Without being ordered, Hannibal ran forward to his gun, already loaded and primed. Then, as the *Fair Molly* sped back down the channel, they caught a glimpse of the enemy schooner. She lay on her side, with her sails awash and the surf of the inlet bar pounding over her.

"Mr. Stilwell," called the captain, "get ready to launch the boat. Whether we want to or not, we've got to save those men."

Nine

The boat carried by the *Fair Molly* was seaworthy but not very large. In fact, it was nothing more than a big fishing dory with places for two rowers.

Will Hand would never forget that nightmare rescue mission. While Aaron and Jonathan did the rowing, he and Matthew Hughes leaned over the side, grabbing at half-drowned sailors who floundered in the surf. Once he had a heavy seaman almost up to the gunwale when the boat pitched and the man's arm slipped from his grasp. Others were more fortunate. A white face would appear alongside in the blackness, and Will would reach down to seize a hand, a collar, even a mop of hair. In all, they hauled six men into the boat, and by then it was overloaded with retching, dripping bodies.

"Don't see any more," Matt gasped. "Let's get 'em back to the sloop."

When all six prisoners were examined for injuries and put below, in the cargo hold, Captain Hand dropped anchor in the channel, a mile above the inlet, and had the sails lowered.

"We'll have to wait for daylight," he said, "to get a better look at their vessel."

The crew took four-hour watches and slept between-times. When dawn began to break, they sailed back to the bar. They could see that the British schooner had righted herself with the morning tide and seemed to be moving a little on the shoal in response to the push of the waves.

At once the skipper moved the sloop closer. A cable's length away, he had the anchor dropped again and ordered the boat launched. "Hannibal," he said, "you an' Jenkins stay here an' guard the prisoners. The rest of us'll go aboard her."

They approached the schooner warily, their muskets held ready. When nobody appeared on her deck, they ran in alongside, shipped their oars, and climbed up the side into the vessel's waist.

She was a pitiful sight, her deck cluttered with a tangle of cordage, her fore-topmast hanging askew, and her rails smashed where her cannon had broken loose and gone over the side.

"See what you can do to clear the deck," Captain Hand told the mate. "I want to go below for a look."

He approached the cabin hatch and disappeared into the companionway while Will watched anxiously.

"Come, boys, get to work!" Amos Stilwell ordered. "Aaron, get aloft an' cut that topmast free. You, Will an' Matt, start coilin' ropes."

They had been at this task only a few minutes when the skipper reappeared. "Nobody left aboard," he announced. "I found her papers, though, an' she's the *Lady Gay*, commissioned by the Royal Navy after bein' captured. She's from down East, a coastin' schooner out o' Bath, Maine. That means she's stout-built. But before we can do anything with her, she's got to have some o' the water pumped out. Two of you get on the pump there, amidships."

Luckily the pump had not been damaged. The two boys put their backs into it—up—down—up—down—while a flood of seawater gushed out through the scuppers. But it was certain to be a long job. Will could hear the slosh of several feet of water in the hold.

After a while Aaron came down from the foremast, and he and the mate took their turns at the pump. Two hours had passed, and the sun was well up when Hannibal hailed them from the sloop. He held up the huge coffeepot to show that breakfast was ready.

"Go eat," Captain Hand told Matt and Will. "But don't waste any time. We've got to get her free on this tide."

The two young crewmen rowed back to the sloop and hurried their breakfast, while Hannibal stood watching operations aboard the schooner.

"She's ridin' higher in the water," he observed. "That pumpin' must be doin' some good. There—the keel's free! She's startin' to move!"

"Come on, Matt, we've got to get back," urged Will.

They swallowed the last of their food and jumped into the boat. When they reached the schooner, she had already drifted several lengths inside the bar.

"Will," said his father, "go aloft with Aaron an' help

straighten out the runnin' riggin'. Matthew, get to work at the pump. I'm goin' below to see if her bottom's leakin' too bad."

High on the masts, the two boys did their best to unsnarl ropes and tackle. The canvas was still wet and heavy but showed no rents. If grounding on the bar hadn't caused too much damage to her hull, Will began to think the *Lady Gay* could be sailed!

Captain Hand came back on deck. "Not a hole I can see anywhere," he said. "Just a seam or two started, is all. She's a stout ship—and our first prize! How about it, boys? Think her sails'll draw now?"

"Aye, aye, sir," answered Aaron smartly. "All clear above, sir."

The skipper looked aloft and nodded. "We'll sail her upchannel," he announced. "Amos, you'd better go back to the sloop an' bring her along after us."

Soon both vessels were anchored two miles to the north, where they were well hidden by the wooded island. There Ezra Hand left Aaron to act as shipkeeper and returned with the others to the sloop.

"We'll have to feed those prisoners," he said. "Bring 'em on deck two at a time, Amos."

The first pair were sullen-looking seamen who scowled at the bowls of fish chowder Hannibal offered them.

"Cor!" said one. "Soup! Ain't ye got a bit of 'ardtack to put some body in it?"

"Eat it!" the big cook ordered sternly.

The hungry sailors took a taste, and their expressions changed as they discovered the flavor of onions, potatoes, and big chunks of fish. When they had gobbled it all, the captain asked them some questions. They said there had been fifteen men aboard the schooner—a young ensign in command, a second officer, a bosun, a quartermaster, and eleven in the crew.

Neither had seen exactly what happened when she struck. But they thought the ensign, the bosun, and two seamen had gotten off in the gig just as the schooner capsized. Several had been crushed by the cannon. And, to Will's amazement, they admitted that only a few of them knew how to swim.

The next couple confirmed their story, except that one of them insisted the ensign had been the last to leave the stricken ship. "She was on 'er beam-ends," he said, "an' all of us thought she'd break up. The mate got bashed by the gun, an' the rest of us was drowndin'. So there was nothin' for Ensign Mason to do but escape if he could."

"Except save some of you," the skipper growled. "We did, you know."

They learned little more from the interrogation. The *Lady Gay* had been in the coasting trade and was captured by the British fleet a few weeks earlier. She was very fast, so Commodore Beresford had put a long gun aboard her and had her lie in wait for the privateer.

One or two of the prisoners seemed mystified by the ease with which the sloop had crossed the bar. "We thought as 'ow we drew no more water than you did," they complained. But the crew of the *Fair Molly* merely smiled and carefully avoided looking at the centerboard.

It was now well along in the afternoon. When the prisoners had been safely returned to the hold, Captain Hand sent Will ashore on the island with Matt Hughes.

"Pick the tallest tree you can find," he said, "an' climb it. There may be some British ships waitin' for us off the inlet. Come back an' tell me anything you see out there."

Will was glad to be given something to do. He and Matt rowed the boat to the inner shore of the island and beached it, then scrambled through the woods toward the beach. A tall tulip poplar caught Will's eye, but the bare trunk offered no hold for a climber's hands, and it was too large around for shinnying.

"Too bad we didn't bring a rope," he told Matt.

"There's one in the boat," his companion replied eagerly. "I saw it when I was rowin'. It's under the stern thwart."

Before Will could answer him, he was racing back the way they had come. When he returned, he was carrying a coil of half-inch manila line, close to a hundred feet long. Will took it from the panting boy and shook out half of it. His first cast missed, but then, with a might heave, he threw the end over a branch, well up the tree. A few flips brought the loose end down, and he had a doubled rope to climb. Up he went, hand over hand.

"Hey, what do you see?" called Matt when he paused at a crotch some fifty feet above the ground.

"Just open ocean all the way to the cape," Will answered. "Not a sail anywhere in sight."

He descended by the same route, coiled the rope, and they made their way back to the boat. Once on board the sloop, Will made his report.

"It's sort o' hard to believe," said the captain. "All I can figure is that the ensign an' his men never made it back to the fleet. If they did, you'd expect some action by now.

Well, we can't stay bottled up in here. Think you can sail the schooner out, Amos?"

The mate looked thoughtful. "Yep," he said. "Give me two good men an' a real flood tide, an' I reckon we can make it."

"All right, take your pick o' the crew."

Stilwell chose Aaron Schellenger and Jonathan Jenkins, and they went aboard the *Lady Gay* to get her ready. The tide wouldn't reach full flood on the bar before ten that night, judging by the morning tide that had floated the schooner. So there was little to do but wait. As darkness came on, Hannibal passed out mugs of coffee to Captain Hand and the two remaining members of his crew. Over on the schooner, the others had found food in the galley and could fend for themselves.

Another two hours passed, and the tide was running strongly up the channel.

"Here we go, Amos," Ezra Hand called. "Reckon you can find the way out. If not, just follow us. You'll have enough water."

They heard a snort from the mate. "I could get out o' Hereford Inlet if I was blindfolded!" he answered.

The skipper chuckled and had the sails hoisted, then weighed anchor. The wind was light and from the west as the *Fair Molly* cruised down-channel toward the inlet. A few hundred yards astern, the schooner followed. Nearing the line of surf on the bar, the captain sent Will up to the masthead.

"I can hold her a minute," he told him. "Holler out quick if there's an enemy sail out there!"

Will scanned the horizon but saw only empty sea. "All

clear!" he shouted, and a moment later the sloop was skimming through the narrow gap in the breakers.

Amos Stilwell proved his own seamanship by bringing the *Lady Gay* out safely. Her crew had set the sails on both masts as well as the jib, and she was moving about as fast as the sloop.

They changed course to the northward as soon as they were clear of the land. Running without lights, Captain Hand led the way up along Seven Mile Beach, past Townsend's Inlet, and onward, with low, brush-covered dunes on the port beam.

Will, still clinging to the crosstrees, watched the sea astern. He expected at any moment to see the square sails of a pursuing ship, but there was only the schooner behind them. He had never sailed along this part of the coast before. However, he was almost certain that his father must be heading for Great Egg Harbor. That, he thought with a thrill of excitement, was where some of the privateers put in with their prizes.

At last the skipper took pity on him and called him down, sending Matt aloft to replace him. It was then well past midnight. Will, who had had little sleep the night before, tumbled into his bunk and knew no more until Hannibal shook him awake at daybreak.

The prisoners were shouting and pounding on the bulkheads below, but Captain Hand paid no attention to them. He was too busy at the helm. They were, as Will could see, entering a broad inlet, with marshy islands to port and a low headland on the starboard side.

"Great Egg," his father told him gruffly.

"Gosh, Dad," Will said anxiously, "I should think you'd be awful tired! Can't I take the tiller a spell?"

"No, thanks. The channel's not easy to find. Once we land these prisoners, I'll sleep the clock 'round."

The mate kept his vessel close in their wake, and by the time the sun was well up, both craft were in the middle of a fairly large bay. Their course was now southwestward as they made for Beesley's Point and the mouth of the Tucka-hoe River.

As they approached the settlement there, an American flag was run up on the sloop's mast, so that they wouldn't be fired on as invading enemies. A small crowd had gathered on the dock when Captain Hand brought the *Fair Molly* in alongside.

A middle-aged man wearing a militia officer's uniform stepped forward out of the knot of bystanders. "That you, Cap'n Hand?" he asked. "I'm Ephraim Willetts, commandin' the Upper Township Battalion. Thought I recognized the old packet, an' I've heard you were privateerin' now. Looks like you've brought in a prize!"

"Glad to see you, Eph," the skipper returned. "Not much of a capture, but we salvaged the schooner when she tried to chase us into Hereford Inlet an' piled herself up on the bar. We pulled six Britishers out o' the water. Hope you've got jail room to take 'em off our hands."

Major Willetts grinned. "I reckon we'll be glad to keep 'em," he said. "An' the schooner's a likely-lookin' craft. Ought to bring a good price. You aim to leave her here?"

"I'd like to," said Will's father. "When's the next government auction?"

"They're supposed to be here in two or three weeks. We've got a couple of other prizes waitin' to be sold. I'll call a squad o' men to take care o' your prisoners."

He went back to one of the houses, and a moment later they heard a bell toll. As if by magic, half a dozen militiamen trotted into view, priming their muskets as they came.

Hannibal had made a kettle of fresh chowder, and as the captives were brought up from the hold, each one was given a pannikin of the steaming stew. When all had been fed, they were marched off under guard, and the *Fair Molly*'s crew heaved a sigh of relief.

It took the rest of the morning to furl the schooner's sails, clear her decks, and moor her close to the bank, in company with the other two captured vessels. After that, as he had promised, Captain Hand went to bed.

"Call me tomorrow at sunup," he told Will. "Mr. Stilwell will be in charge till then."

That evening the mate gave the youthful crew permission to go ashore, with the understanding that they must be back aboard before midnight.

"Say, Will," said Matt, "I know a couple o' girls that live here in Beesley's Point. Come on—let's go callin'!"

The pair put on clean shirts, combed and slicked their hair, and went up the road to the big house where Micajah Stites lived. He had two pert daughters named Jane and Ellen, and they were delighted to entertain the two young sailors from the other end of the country. But in the middle of the evening, after the boys had eaten their fill of molasses cookies and drunk at least a gallon of lemonade, Will nudged Matt.

"What say we go back to the sloop?" he whispered. One more glass o' lemonade an' I won't be able to climb the riggin' tomorrow."

So ended their first shore leave in a strange port.

Ten

There was an air of tense expectancy aboard the *Fair Molly* when they sailed her out of Great Egg Harbor early in the morning. It was a fine, clear day, and the newly risen sun was bright on the sea.

Will had been sent aloft to his usual post at the masthead. He watched the southern horizon sharply, but there was no sign of any ship. As they crossed the entrance bar, his father ordered the main sheet close-hauled and tacked the sloop northward into a freshening breeze. He had made no announcement of his plans, but Will was sure this must mean a foray up the coast toward Brigantine or Barnegat.

They beat their way past the sandy shore of Absecon Island. It was when they were nearing Absecon Inlet that Will spied a dot of sail far ahead. He hailed the deck to report it, but his father did nothing except to coax more speed out of the sloop. An hour later they had gained on the other vessel. Will could make out her rigging now. She was a brig, he decided—a fat-hulled, lumbering craft with weathered brown sails.

Amos Stilwell examined her through the spyglass and confirmed Will's judgment. "Looks like a furriner," he commented. "Comes from the West Indies, maybe."

"Good enough," the captain said. "Run up the flag, boys. An' you, Hannibal, get your gun ready for action. She's probably carryin' supplies to the fleet off New York."

The chase grew more exciting now. They could see extra sails being set on the brig, which appeared to be making far less progress to windward than the sloop. There was no flag visible, and Will was certain she would have broken out the Stars and Stripes if she had been a friendly ship.

They were off Little Egg Inlet when they caught up with the larger vessel. No gunports could be seen in her sides, and only a few seamen's heads showed above her rail. Ezra Hand turned the helm over to the mate and brought a speaking trumpet from the cabin.

"Ahoy, the brig!" he bellowed. "Show your colors if you're American!"

There was no answering hail, and they saw the brig attempt to wear off to seaward.

"Heave to!" roared the skipper. "Quick, now, before I open fire on you!"

Slowly and reluctantly, with a creaking of spars, the brig came about into the wind and rocked there with her sails flapping. Will was told to come down to the deck.

"Man the gun," the captain ordered. "You, Aaron an' Will, get the boat over. I'm goin' to board her."

The two young sailors took muskets with them and low-

ered the boat over the side. As Ezra Hand climbed down to take the stern thwart, he gave a final command.

"If you see 'em put up anything that looks like a fight," he said, "fire point-blank. But don't hit her below the waterline. She's no good to us if she's sunk."

Facing aft as he rowed, Will felt a prickling sensation in the back of his neck, for he wondered each second if a bullet might come from the brig. His father's face appeared unperturbed, however, and back on the sloop, it was comforting to see Hannibal standing by the breach of the nine-pounder, slow match in hand.

They covered the short distance quickly.

"Ship your oars," said Captain Hand. "Hold her here by the ladder while I go aboard."

Will saw that the crew of the brig had indeed dropped a rope ladder over the side, and up it his father climbed briskly. It was impossible to hear what was said on the deck above them, but at least there were no shots or outcries. After four or five minutes, the captain reappeared at the rail.

"They've surrendered," he told the boys calmly. "Shouldn't have any trouble." Then he cupped his hands and called to Stilwell to bring the sloop nearer. When she lay hove to, a hundred feet away, Aaron was told to come up the ladder while Will rowed back to get the mate.

"Amos," said Captain Hand, when his first officer arrived, "you've sailed squareriggers before. I want you to take command an' follow the sloop into Great Bay. You can have these two men an' Matt Jenkins. I'm takin' her captain an' mate back to the *Fair Molly*, but the crew are blacks from the Bahamas. They've got no special love for the British, an' they'll give you no trouble."

The captain of the brig was a sallow, worried-looking man named Windham, who came meekly down the ladder. The mate, a big, scowling fellow, followed under the prodding of Ezra Hand's pistol muzzle, and the boys rowed them to the sloop. As soon as the prisoners were confined in the hold, they brought Matt back with them and made their boat fast astern of the brig.

The crew stood about looking scared and bewildered, but they did snap to attention when Stilwell gave an order.

"Haul those yards," he told them. "We're goin' about."

He himself took the wheel, and all the three boys had to do was watch the crew, with their muskets held ready. In a few minutes the brig was wallowing along in the wake of the *Fair Molly*. She seemed to handle better before the wind. The entrance into Great Bay was made without difficulty, and by midafternoon the two vessels were well into the broad mouth of the Mullica River.

The place where they finally dropped anchor was off Lower Bank. Captain Hand was rowed back aboard the prize, where he congratulated his mate.

"Could be a right good haul, Amos," he said. "Come on into the cabin with me an' we'll look over her papers."

It turned out that the captured brig was the *Carlotta*, out of Nassau. She was carrying a cargo of sugar, molasses, and rum, consigned to the British blockade fleet off New York.

"Near as I can figure," said the skipper, "she must have close to ten thousand dollars' worth o' cargo aboard! We may have to wait a month or so before she's sold, but I'll fix it to have the militia take over the prisoners an' see to it that the brig's safe here."

He had Will and Matt row him ashore to the village dock. A few curious youngsters came down to the pier to ask about the brig and her capture.

"We're off the privateer sloop out yonder," Will told them. "Took her without firin' a shot. That's our second prize in less'n three days," he couldn't help bragging.

"Well, well," said the oldest of the boys. "You don't look so durn desp'rit. Was the other ship as easy as this 'un?"

"She was a British Navy armed schooner," Will replied hotly. "Carried more'n double the men we did, an—"

A sudden voice interrupted from the dock. "That's enough, boy," growled Will's father. "I'll do the talkin' if any's to be done."

During the trip back to the *Fair Molly*, he had some further words for Will. "There's some old Tory feelin' amongst a few o' the folks 'round here," he said. "The less they know, the better, so don't go braggin' about what we've done. It could get us in trouble."

Hannibal went ashore later to buy fresh eggs and other provisions. And almost as soon as he returned, a whaleboat manned by militiamen came to the sloop. They took the brig's officers and crew back to the village lockup and promised to notify the federal authorities.

"The government's anxious to get prisoners to exchange," the lieutenant explained. "I hope they'll come for 'em right away, for we don't have jail room for more'n the captain an' mate. The blacks'll have to sleep in the stockade, outside."

Captain Hand and Amos Stilwell talked over plans and

decided there was nothing to be gained by staying at Lower Bank.

"If we wait for the brig to be sold," Will's father said, "we might be tied up here till September. So we'll sneak out tonight an' try to make it home before daylight."

Will had wondered about the Negro crew, and knowing Hannibal had talked to them, he asked him about them that afternoon.

"They're from a British island, right enough," the cook told him. "But they ain't free. Near's I could make out from that funny lingo they talk, their master hired 'em out to be crew for this Cap'n Windham. Down there in the Bahamas, most black boys are around boats from the time they can walk, so they make good sailors. One of 'em let on to me they wasn't too sorry to be took prisoner after bein' slaves all their lives. That ugly mate heard a little of it an' wanted to shut the man up, but I had a gun an' he didn't."

Hannibal chuckled at the recollection. "Didn't like that feller from the minute I seen him," he added.

As darkness fell, they readied the sloop for sea and dropped down the Mullica into Great Bay. An east wind made it necessary to tack out past the islands, and it was getting on toward midnight when they reached the open sea. Once clear of the land, however, the wind came from abeam, and they had a reach all the way down the coast.

Under full sail the *Fair Molly* heeled over and showed what she could do. They were making better than ten knots, Will thought, as he clung to his lookout post in the crosstrees. It was a clear night, and there were no sails on the horizon, so he had time to do some mental arithmetic. His father, as sole owner of the privateer, would take a quarter of all the prize money they might make after the government had taken its half. Of the rest, he figured Amos Stilwell would receive a double share. But each of the remaining members of the crew might expect two hundred dollars or more! That was far more money than Will had ever possessed in his life.

They sped on down past Absecon and Great Egg Inlet, past Corson's Inlet and Townsend's Inlet. Still no sail had appeared. Finally they were below Seven Mile Beach, and it was still dark. Just as the first gray light struck the eastern sea, the sloop turned to starboard, making for Cold Spring Inlet. They were home and safe!

✹   ✹   ✹

With his father's permission, Will didn't wait for breakfast aboard the sloop. He wanted to get home to the farm.

The girls were washing the dishes when he entered the kitchen door, but as soon as he called a greeting, Martha Hand came hurrying out to prepare his breakfast.

"Did you have any adventures?" his sisters asked. "Did you capture any prizes?"

He looked around to make certain Roger Thornhill was out of hearing. "Only two," he replied casually. "Took the first one into the Tuckahoe an' the second to Lower Bank. We got quite a few prisoners, but there wasn't any fightin' to speak of."

Lovey stood there with her mouth open, but Faith was less impressed. "Don't sound as if you had much fun," she said with a sniff.

"Oh, well," Will told her, "Matt Jenkins an' I did go

callin' on a couple o' girls, up at Beesley's Point. Rich ones, too, I reckon. Lived in a big, fancy house. Name o' Stites."

"They'd be Micajah Stites's daughters," his mother said with a nod. "Plenty o' money there, I guess. Hope you minded your manners, Willing."

He didn't tell them about leaving early. As soon as he had reassured them about his father's health, he fell to eating the huge breakfast that was set before him. When he had finished, he went out to the barn. It looked as if the two girls had done a good job, for the stalls were clean and the pigs and chickens seemed well fed and happy. Back in the pasture, the cows were grazing, and the old mare had been turned out to join them.

The only animal that acted restless was his own black colt. Prince snorted, pricked up his ears, and pawed the plank floor at sight of his master.

"You'll have to wait, boy," Will told the young horse. "I got work to do 'fore I can go ridin'."

He took a hoe and went out to the cornfield, where the stalks now stood shoulder high and a few tassels had begun to appear. There was little for him to do there, for the corn's shade had killed off the weeds. He moved on to the potato patch, where some hoeing was really needed. It was warm and pleasant, and the sweet whistling of bobwhite quail came across the fields. A deep sense of contentment filled him, and he leaned on his hoe, wiping the sweat from his forehead.

"Too hot to work?" a voice asked behind him.

Startled, Will whirled about and saw a square-shouldered young man in a worn gray coat standing there look-

ing at him. He wasn't exactly smiling, but his rugged face was pleasant enough.

"No, the weather's all right," Will answered. "Just felt like a minute's rest, I reckon."

"This your farm?"

"My father's. You lookin' for him?"

"That depends. What's your father's name?"

"Ezra Hand. You got business with him?"

"Maybe so. The Hand I'm looking for is more of a sailor than a farmer. Used to be a Delaware Bay pilot, I believe. He's likely given up the sea now that the Delaware's under blockade."

Will didn't answer directly, but he nodded and used his bandanna to hide a grin. "Dad may be home pretty soon," he said. "I'll walk you back to the house if you want. This work'll keep."

The man walked with a rolling stride that told Will better than words that he was accustomed to pacing a ship's deck. He didn't speak like a Jerseyman, either. Perhaps, he thought with a shock, he was moving beside a spy from the British fleet. But his common sense refused to accept that idea.

"You mind tellin' me your name?" Will asked.

"Not a bit. I'm John Morris."

"Don't live 'round here, do you?"

"No—I come from Philadelphia."

Will let the information rest there. He doubted if Mr. Morris would tell him much more, and he was satisfied to let his father find out the man's mission.

They reached the farmyard just as Captain Hand came

in from the road. He caught sight of the pair and stopped where he was.

"Dad," Will called. "This is Mr. Morris from Philadelphia. He's come down here to see you."

The skipper's face lit up. "Jack Morris!" he cried. "Well, I'll be hornswoggled!"

Will stood there with his eyes popping while his father pumped the stranger's hand.

"You still in the Navy, boy?" he asked. "What brings you down here to the cape?"

"Came to see you, of course. I've been told you still own the old sloop and that nobody knows the creeks and inlets as well as you do."

"I ain't one to brag," the captain told him, "but some o' that's true, I guess. Jack, I can't talk to you much in the house 'cause we've got a young British prisoner Martha's nursin'. I've got to report in to her, but I'll see you in the barn pretty quick. Will, you show him the way an' see that he's comfortable!"

Eleven

Now that Will knew who their visitor was, he had no more qualms about answering questions. He told how the *Fair Molly* had first been turned into a packet boat, then into a privateer. Giving full credit to the luck that had favored them, he described the short voyage they had just completed.

"We took plenty o' prisoners, anyhow," he said. "More'n a dozen in all, an' six of 'em were British Navy men. The ensign in command o' their schooner an' three others got away in the gig. We thought sure they'd have the fleet down on us when we tried to come out o' Hereford Inlet."

"I think I can explain that," said Morris. "The gig had a plank stove in and was leaking faster than they could bail. They finally went ashore on Five Mile Beach. Two militiamen were on patrol there, and they captured them all."

"Gee!" Will said in astonishment. "How'd you hear that?"

Morris chuckled. "Hearing things is my job. I was down at Cape Island last night before your sloop showed up."

It wasn't until Ezra Hand came out of the house, a short time later, that the young Naval officer revealed his real mission. He had been sent to scout the Jersey shore of Delaware Bay and the various rivers and inlets. To do it properly, he needed to charter a boat and a good pilot.

"I hear you've had a pretty good cruise as a privateer," he said. "Now here's another way to serve your country."

The skipper thought it over. " 'Twon't be easy," he commented. "First we've got to get the sloop around the cape an' past the British fleet. How much does the Navy want to pay?"

"I'm allowed to spend up to a hundred dollars to get the job done. You might make a lot more on a lucky voyage, but, as I said, this is for the United States."

Captain Hand nodded. "We'll take you," he said. "Reckon you won't mind if we pick up a few oysters an' such to help pay for the trip?"

"Not a bit," Morris replied with a chuckle. "It'll give us a good excuse for going into some of these places. How soon can you start?"

"S'pose we say tomorrow evening at first dark," said Ezra Hand. "You meet us down at the Cold Spring dock. I'll ship you on as a first-class seaman, if that suits you."

"Just what I'd have suggested," Morris answered. "There's one other thing I meant to ask. Do you have any British sympathizers here in the county? Somebody, we figure, is getting word about ship movements to that fleet in the bay."

Will exchanged a glance with his father, who thought a moment before he answered.

"We've had some suspicions here," he said guardedly. "Lieutenant Townsend said he'd look into it. You might ask him if you run into him. Now, how about havin' dinner with us?"

"No, Ezra, I'd better not show myself to your prisoner. I've no doubt he's all right, but we can't take any risks. Thank you, and I'll be at the dock tomorrow night."

When he had gone, Will began asking questions. John Morris, he learned, had been a young Navy ensign aboard a harbor patrol boat when Captain Hand was piloting ships up the river, and they had seen each other often. He was a Philadelphian now, but he came originally from Gloucester, in New Jersey. That was probably why he had been given this assignment.

"Anyhow," said Ezra Hand, "we won't lose money by it, just so we stay afloat."

"You plan to take the whole crew, Dad?"

"No, I reckon they'll welcome a spell ashore, since there's no prizes to be taken. Just you an' Hannibal an' Jack Morris ought to make all the crew we need."

"What about the nine-pounder?" Will asked. "Think we're likely to have to use it?"

"I've thought about that," his father replied. "It shows up like a sore thumb, there on the foredeck. If we're goin' to act like a peaceful packet sloop, we'd better leave the gun ashore. You ride up to the militia camp this afternoon an' ask Josh Townsend if he'll send a squad to take it off an' keep it in a safe place."

By the time Will had the colt steadied down, he made the distance to the patch of woods near Town Bank at a good clip. This time no sentry challenged him, and he rode straight into the clearing where the troops had bivouacked. All was silent and deserted there. The militia company had moved somewhere else.

As he sat there in the saddle wondering how to find them, he thought he saw something move, off to his right. It was just a brief glimpse he had had, out of the corner of his eye, and now the woods seemed as still and lonely as ever. Gathering the reins, he urged the colt in that direction, but the underbrush was too thick to let them through. After a moment's indecision, he rode out of the woods the way he had come. Back on the old Bay Road, he headed north toward Fishing Creek. Swain's store was one place where he thought he could get news of Josh Townsend's movements.

Riding along, he glanced back to his left, still bothered by the thing he fancied he had seen moving. The woods were a long way off now, but where a field met the trees, a dark figure was dodging through the shadows. The distance was too great to be sure of the man's shape, but in his own mind Will believed it was Ferd Leech, spying again.

He entered the village and stopped at Swain's. The storekeeper himself sat rocking on the narrow porch. Business appeared to be slow.

"Well, young Hand," he greeted Will, "you ain't here to tell me you got another shipment for me, are you?"

"No, sir." Will laughed. "Just thought you might be

117

able to tell me where I can find Lieutenant Townsend o' the militia."

"I might." Mr. Swain looked furtively up and down the road. "Better come inside," he added.

Tying the colt, Will followed him into the store.

"I hear," said the storekeeper in a low voice, "they've moved their camp south. Some way the British found out where they were an' sent a gunboat to fire a few shots into the woods. Right now my guess is you'd find 'em down near Cape May P'int—somewheres back o' the Lily Pond."

Will thanked him, bought his usual licorice stick, and rode southward again. He knew the area Swain had described, but he didn't want to make his approach too obvious. When he had crossed the little bridge over Pond Creek, he hitched Prince to a sapling and went on afoot.

The Lily Pond was a spring-fed pool of fresh water, west of the lighthouse on Cape May Point. Earlier in the war, British boats had come there regularly to fill their water barrels. But some angry residents had dug a long ditch, letting the tide into the pond and making it too salty to drink.

There were only one or two homes along the sandy road. After the last one Will came to marshy ground, where the tall canes of bulrushes made a dense screen, a dozen feet tall. Watching as he walked, he spied a tiny opening, almost as narrow as a rabbit path. He entered it cautiously, and before he had gone ten steps, a gruff voice told him to halt. There was a homespun-clad soldier a yard or two away, pointing a musket at his chest.

"All right, Luke," said Will, "you know I'm no enemy,

even if I can't give you the password. All I want is a minute to talk to Josh Townsend. Is he around?"

The young militiaman recognized him. "March in front o' me, Will," he answered. "I got to say I'm bringin' in a prisoner."

The twisting little path led another hundred feet through the high reeds and emerged suddenly on a small patch of higher ground, clear of brush. Twenty or thirty men were stretched out there, resting, but they reached for their guns when Will and the sentry appeared.

"Oh, it's you again, Will Hand," one of them said with relief. "There's the lieutenant yonder, if you're lookin' for him."

Josh Townsend grinned at the sight of him. "Go back to your post, Foster," he told the guard. "What can I do for the Hand family?"

It took Will only a few words to deliver his father's message, and when he finished, Townsend nodded.

"We'll get over there tonight," he said. "Giving up privateering?"

"Not for long, I reckon. Dad's got a special job to do."

"I must say I envied you, being at sea," the lieutenant said, slapping at a mosquito. "This may be a snug hiding place, but the bugs are pretty hungry."

It was unusual for a Jerseyman to admit his skin wasn't too tough for mosquitoes, but as he looked about, Will saw vast swarms of the insects coming in from the marsh. He somehow doubted if the militia would spend much more time there.

"Just one other thing," he said before he left. "We'll

need to know where the British ships are when we're ready to leave."

"Sure," said Townsend. "We keep a lookout over in the dunes, and he'll signal us in time to let you know."

Will took his leave then and walked back through the reeds to the road. He waited to make sure no one was in sight before he stepped out. Ten minutes later he had re-mounted the colt and was on his way home. He reached the farm not long before suppertime.

＊　　＊　　＊

After the evening chores were done, Will and his father left the house.

"May be home a little late," Ezra Hand told his wife, and she nodded gloomily. Will thought she must often wish for a normal, landlubber husband, who kept depend-able hours.

The crew was still aboard the sloop, and the skipper called them all into the cabin. "You boys have done fine," he told them, "and I don't want to lose you in case we make another privateerin' cruise. Right now, though, the sloop's needed for a different kind o' work. All I can tell you is that it's a government order. So stay handy, an' I'll let you know when to report again. You're still signed on, an' this is just a kind o' shore leave."

Their curiosity was natural, but they had to be satisfied with what he told them. Half an hour after they had left, Will heard the creak of wagon wheels and saw a group of men approaching.

Lieutenant Townsend's squad worked quickly and quietly. The cannon was eased onto the dock and lifted to the wagon bed. Then, with a few whispered words, they departed, taking the gun with them.

Ezra Hand explained the new plan to Hannibal, then left him to guard the sloop. By ten-thirty both Will and his father were home in bed.

It was one of the chilly nights that August sometimes brings to the seashore, and Will snuggled under the covers. He was far less tense over the coming trip than he had been before their privateer venture. This, he thought, would be no more dangerous than an ordinary packet trip. So he went to sleep at once.

The day dawned crisp and bright. There was no frost, for the nearness of the sea tempered the morning air. But Will didn't dawdle over getting into his clothes.

"Might as well finish up the potato patch," his father suggested to him when he went out to the barn. "Nothin' much else to do till dark. If we hung around the sloop, it might make folks curious."

Will spent most of his day hoeing potatoes, but he didn't mind. The air was cooled by a westerly breeze, and he had the prospect of the voyage up the Delaware to think about. John Morris was to be his shipmate, and he liked and admired the young Naval officer.

In the middle of the afternoon, he was surprised to see Roger Thornhill coming across the field. The midshipman's wound had healed rapidly, and he looked fit enough, in spite of his indoor pallor.

"I thought a bit of work would be good for me," he told Will with a smile. "One gets bored with sitting about. You see, I've even brought a hoe!"

"That's fine!" said Will. "Ever done any o' this before?"

"Not potatoes," Roger admitted. "But we had a garden plot at home where I sometimes worked. Your sister Lovey says you'll be going to sea again after today."

Will stiffened and glanced at him quickly, but the smooth young face was innocent enough.

"Yep," he answered casually. "Just another market trip. But we'll try to stay clear o' your blockade ships."

The young Englishman flushed at the words. "It's odd," he said quietly, "but I don't feel as if they were my ships now. Perhaps I'm becoming a colonial."

Will chuckled and shook his head. "You folks are slow to learn," he said. "This country stopped bein' a colony some time back. But I take it as a compliment that you feel at home here."

They hoed in silence for a time. Then Roger stopped and stood listening. "What sort of bird is that singing?" he asked.

"That? Oh, just an old redwing blackbird. There's thousands of 'em 'round here."

"It's a sweet song, though, with that little trill in it," said Roger. "I've heard it many times from my bedroom. Does the bird really have red wings?"

"Just a shoulder patch," Will told him. "Look—there's one now."

Roger stood entranced, watching and listening to the singer. "You have so many strange creatures here!" he said. "I learn something new every day."

As suppertime neared, they went back to the house together. Will felt closer to this stranger from another land than ever before.

❂   ❂   ❂

There was a small new moon in the western sky, but it did little to dispel the dark that hung over the dock at Cold Spring Inlet. The sloop lay there rocking gently to

123

the ripple of the tide, and the only sign of life was the long, muscular form of Hannibal, stretched out on the fore-hatch.

Will and his father had left home quietly after the evening chores were done. The captain had given Lieutenant Morris no exact time for departure, so now he took Hannibal with him to the cabin to explain matters while they waited. Will leaned on the rail and watched the shoreline.

"All ready to cast off?" asked a low voice at his elbow, and, startled, he whirled about to see who had spoken. To his amazement John Morris stood there smiling.

"How—how'd you get aboard?" he whispered. "I was lookin' at the dock the whole time!"

"It's easy enough in the dark," the lieutenant told him. "I could see you were watching, so I just came in from another direction. Where's your father?"

"In the cabin. I'll get him."

In a moment he was back, bringing the captain, who shook hands with their passenger.

"I figured on waitin' till the moon was down," he said. "But we can use the time to plan a little. Any word about the fleet?"

Morris nodded. "The *Poictiers* and one frigate sailed south two days ago. Only a couple of smaller ships left on patrol."

"All right," said the captain. "Ought to make it easier. Will, get ready to hoist sail. We'll leave in half an hour."

Twelve

It was pitch dark when the *Fair Molly* went out through Cold Spring Inlet. The tide was well over the bar, and their passage was easy. Morris, Will found, was an excellent seaman, and they worked smoothly together, hauling up the mainsail, topsail, and jib. Once outside, with her centerboard down, the sloop heeled over on the starboard tack to beat her way around the point of the cape.

If the ships left on guard at the mouth of the Delaware were carrying riding lights, they were too far away to be seen. Ezra Hand had sent Will aloft on lookout duty, while the Navy man minded the sheet. For twenty minutes the sloop beat to windward. She was on the port tack as she rounded Cape May Point, and the skipper was ready to put the helm over for the northward reach when Will saw the dark loom of sails off to the west. Some kind of vessel was bearing down on them. Hastily he hailed the deck.

"What do you make her out to be?" asked Captain Hand calmly. "An' how far off?"

"Looks like a schooner," Will replied. "Less'n half a mile, I'd judge."

His father swung the tiller, and the *Fair Molly* heeled over a bit farther as she skimmed north along the coast. She was only a few hundred yards from the surf line. The other vessel was also changing course, and it was obvious now that she had sighted the sloop.

Will hardly needed to announce that they were being chased, for the red flash of a cannon and the booming report that followed made it all too evident.

"Come down, boy!" shouted the captain. "An' get ready to repel boarders!"

Those were brave words, but Will couldn't help wondering if they would be shot to pieces first. He scrambled down to the deck, took his loaded rifle, and joined John Morris and Hannibal by the port rail.

The first shot had missed, but the schooner was close astern now, and the next one might rip the hull. The thought had barely crossed Will's mind when another cannon roared from a different direction. This shot came from the shore!

"Reckon that may be Josh Townsend takin' a hand," said the skipper. "He told me he might find use for that long nine of ours. I'd give somethin' to know how the British found out we'd be here, though."

"The schooner's acting queer," the lieutenant put in. "Look—by thunder I believe she's hit!"

It was true. They could see the pursuing craft falter and

swing head to wind, her sails flapping. Then, with a crashing sound, her main-topmast fell, fouling the fore rigging.

"Don' know who aimed that shot," Hannibal drawled, "but he's a gunner, sure 'nough—or else mighty lucky!"

"Well," said Ezra Hand, "I guess we can go on about our business. Better head a little more to windward, though. There's a few shoals off here."

They sailed northward past such well-remembered inlets as Cox Hall Creek, Fishing Creek, and Green Creek, with the skipper steering by feel and instinct. Some time before midnight they approached the wider mouth of Dennis Creek, and at Morris's request the sloop put in there.

"I'd just like to see if our armed galleys could be hidden here safely," he told Captain Hand. "How much water is there?"

"Fair-sized craft can sail all the way to Dennis. That's four miles inland, an' there's a couple o' fathoms all the way."

The lieutenant seemed pleased. "All right," he said. "Let's go on."

As the coast curved, they had to make a beat of it to the westward. The widest part of the bay was now behind them, and there was no sign of any blockade ship that far north. Hannibal brought tin mugs of coffee to help them stay awake, and the sloop sailed steadily on.

After a brief inspection of the mouth of Maurice River, Captain Hand brought the *Fair Molly* about for the southwest reach, to skirt Egg Island Point. Once around it, they headed north again with the wind on the port beam.

"We'll put into the Cohansey," Will's father said, "an'
go up to Greenwich. Maybe I can load some oysters there.
With luck we ought to be in the river by daylight."

The westerly breeze held, and the voyage proceeded
with no disturbing incident. Then, when they were nearing the Cohansey and Will was having difficulty keeping
his eyes open, Morris hailed the skipper.

"Sail off the port bow!" he called.

There was enough light now to show them the white
canvas of a frigate, coming downwind fast.

"It's all right, Cap'n," said the Navy man. "She's the
Wasp—the Yankee ship that keeps station off Bombay
Hook. I'll just run up our colors so she'll know what we
are."

As soon as the American flag was hoisted, the frigate
dipped her own colors and bore off to the westward.

"She's on the job, right enough." Lieutenant Morris
chuckled. "I'll give her a good report when I get to Philadelphia."

They headed into the Cohansey River just as the sun
was rising. After a half hour's sailing, the captain brought
the sloop smartly in beside a dock at old Greenwich. There
was no one in sight when Will made the mooring line fast
to a bollard. Then an elderly man came limping out of a
nearby shed, rubbing his eyes as he stared at the *Fair
Molly*.

"Ezry?" he asked in a quavering voice. "Is that really
you?"

Will's father laughed. "Yes, sir, Jubal!" he answered.
"Things have been a mite touchy down the bay. But I took

128

a chance an' thought I'd come up an' see if you've been workin' your oyster beds."

"Ain't many men left to man the boats," the oldster told him. "But I reckon we can find a bar'l or two."

"That's good to hear. Come on aboard an' have some breakfast."

Hannibal had been at work in the galley, and now he produced ham and eggs, fried pies, and plenty of strong, black coffee. While they ate, old Jubal eyed Morris with obvious curiosity.

"See ye got a new crewman," he hinted. "Hard to find in wartimes, ain't they?"

"Yep. We were lucky to get John, here. Good sailor, too. Here—have another fried pie."

When they had finished breakfast, the old oysterman led them to his storage shed. "Got ten barrels from yesterday's catch," he said. "All good an' fresh. I'll sell ye some ice, too, if ye want it."

Ezra Hand haggled a bit over the price and finally reached a satisfactory figure. Then Will, Morris, and Hannibal rolled the oyster barrels aboard, shoveling half a ton of broken ice into the hold around them.

The little town was beginning to come to life. Two or three men came shambling down to the oyster boats, tied up along the pier. And up on the road a handful of militiamen went marching westward in a ragged line.

"Goin' to our fortifications," old Jubal remarked with a wink. Neither Will nor his father understood what he meant, but Morris smiled and nodded. "We'll get a better look at them now that the sun's well up," he said.

They cast off the mooring lines and made sail. As they

neared the mouth of the river, Lieutenant Morris pointed toward the higher ground on the northern bank. Will stared at what he saw there. A line of earthworks extended for a hundred yards, and the black muzzles of big guns thrust out in a grim row above the ramparts.

"Quite a battery, isn't it?" asked the Navy officer. "You can see why no British ships have tried to enter the Cohansey."

"Looks mighty strong, for a fact," said the captain. "Wonder where they got all those big cannon."

"Well," the lieutenant said with a laugh, "don't tell anybody, but those are 'Quaker' guns—logs of wood painted to look like forty-pounders. If they fooled you at this distance, it isn't likely the enemy knows any better."

"Wouldn't they think it was a trick, though, if they didn't see any men?" asked Will.

"There's always half a dozen or more on duty here," Morris answered. "And I hear they rigged up a bunch of scarecrows to look like soldiers the last time the British came near. These Cohansey men have plenty of imagination!"

"They sure have! All that would worry me would be a spy, like we have down our way."

"I don't blame you," the Navy man answered seriously. "But we think you've got the only one there is in Cape May County."

The captain sailed the *Fair Molly* boldly out into the bay and headed her for Philadelphia. Three or four miles to the west they could see the *Wasp*, still on guard duty.

The wind was fair from the Delaware shore, and the

sloop logged a steady eight or nine knots as she cruised northward. They were in the river now. Well before noon they sighted the spires of old New Castle. Then they passed Wilmington and Chester, made their way through the booms, and by five o'clock they were threading through the shipping of Philadelphia port.

With his perishable cargo of oysters to think of, Ezra Hand headed directly for the Dock Street Market. And as soon as they had made a mooring, he went ashore to visit the oyster merchants.

John Morris also left the sloop. "I won't be long," he told Will. "I have to report to Captain Evans, but I'll be back to see you and your father this evening."

They missed his strong back when it came time to unload the cargo, but Will and Hannibal managed to heave the barrels to the dock. The man who had bought them was an old customer, and he rubbed his hands with pleasure over buying a shipment of fine Cohansey oysters. They were a rarity in the market in those days, and he gladly paid a price that surprised Will.

When the cargo was unloaded and the skipper had the money in his pocket, he asked where Morris had gone. The explanation satisfied him, and he told Hannibal to go ahead with supper. They were just sitting down to their meal when the young lieutenant returned.

He had been hurrying, and his face was grave. "Bad news," he said, panting. "A courier just brought it from Baltimore. The British have come up the Potomac and landed an army on the Maryland side. They beat our troops at Bladensburg and then marched into Washington, where they burned our new Capitol! Admiral Cockburn's going to attack Baltimore next! And if he wins there, you can wager the whole fleet'll be coming up the Delaware!"

The captain looked at him grimly. "Reckon burnin' the Capitol's about the surest way to get our Yankee dander up," he remarked. "That may be the worst mistake the redcoats have made. You aim to stay here, Lieutenant, or will you go back with us?"

"My orders are to rejoin my ship," Morris replied. "But after seeing how things stand in Cape May County, I'm not worried about your being able to defend yourselves. Only one thing—I hope you catch that spy that's passing information to the enemy! Good luck to all of you!"

He took his seabag and left them sitting there aboard the sloop.

"Things are gettin' serious," Ezra Hand told his son. "I aim to lay in a supply o' things we might need an' then head back home as fast as wind an' tide'll take us."

❖　　❖　　❖

Will slept badly in his bunk that night. He had seen pictures of the wonderful new Capitol building in Washington, and like all good Americans, he thought of it as a symbol of the young republic. Now his heart burned with resentment against this ruthless enemy. The war, so far, had been a sort of game to him, but this news changed it to a life-and-death struggle for the nation's existence. When he finally fell asleep, he dreamed of wrestling with a red-coated soldier who waved a blazing torch.

132

As soon as the shops were open in the morning, Ezra Hand went ashore to buy sugar, salt, needles, and thread. Just about everything else they needed could be supplied by the farm.

High tide came at ten o'clock, and before it turned, the *Fair Molly* was under sail. They left behind them, on the docks and in the streets, a city buzzing with preparations for defense. Some of the shopkeepers were even loading their goods on wagons, ready to flee inland.

The captain chuckled. "Might think all the British wanted was barrels o' pickles an' bolts o' cotton cloth," he said. "I hope folks down Cape May way show more sense."

Crews in galleys were out strengthening the chain booms in the river, but they let the sloop pass, greeting the American flag she flew with a cheer. In midafternoon they were nearing Bombay Hook when they heard a sound of cannon fire ahead. Will was sent up the mast at once.

What he saw from that height sent a tingle of excitement down his spine. A United States frigate, probably the *Wasp*, was hotly engaged with a pair of smaller British vessels—a brig and a schooner. When he called this news down to the deck, his father hove to at once and came aloft with the spyglass.

"She's givin' 'em all they want!" exclaimed the captain. "There—look at that broadside! The brig's done for now, an' t'other one's turned tail. Looked to me like the schooner had a jury main-topmast. So she's prob'ly the same one that chased us night before last."

Even without the aid of the telescope, Will could see the havoc aboard the brig. Her mainmast was gone, and men were scrambling like ants about the cluttered deck. If she still had any guns able to fire, it was impossible to bring them to bear. The frigate left her wallowing there and took off in pursuit of the schooner. Under full sail, the American ship was fast, and both vessels were soon hull-down to the southward.

Ezra Hand climbed down and took the helm again. "We'll keep well over to the Jersey side," he told Will. "Gettin' in range o' that brig's guns would be as bad as foolin' with a wounded bear."

They skirted the mouth of the Cohansey, under the protection of the menacing "guns" mounted there, and were soon well to the south of the damaged British vessel. A faint booming of cannon reached them from down the bay.

"Sounds like the Yankee's caught her," Will's father remarked. "That ought to discourage 'em from comin' up this way again for a while."

An hour later they sighted the frigate again. She was sailing north. There were a couple of rents in her foretopsail, but otherwise she appeared to have come out of the battle unscathed.

"Sure is pretty to see that flag flyin' high!" said Will. "I just wish I'd been aboard her!"

"Don't know as you'd like Navy life," his father replied. "It's mostly a lot o' hard work an' mighty tough discipline. The food ain't as good as Hannibal cooks, either."

They had passed too far to leeward to hail the frigate, but there was something triumphant in the proud way she sailed up the Delaware. In his own mind, at least, Will was sure she had sunk the British schooner.

Sunset came, and they were below Egg Island Point, nearing the upper shores of their own home county. Then darkness fell, but the moon, a little larger now, gave them a good view of the lower bay.

There were no blockade ships to be seen that night.

Thirteen

It was well past midnight when the *Fair Molly* stole into
Cold Spring Inlet and was tied up to the dock. A young
militiaman came out of the shadows to inspect the sloop.

"I see it's you, Cap'n Hand," he said. "We're ordered to
be extra careful. Any news from the city?"

Briefly the captain told him about the burning of Washington. Then he asked the young soldier if he had heard
any firing.

"I thought I did, 'long in the afternoon," he said. "But it
must ha' been quite a ways off. Why—were they shootin'
at you?"

"Not us! It was an American frigate firin' at an armed
schooner the British had sent up toward Bombay Hook.
He may have sunk her."

"Schooner, eh? You reckon it was the same one that near
got you folks t'other night?"

"Looked like the same one. Were you watchin' when she chased us? Tell me—who was it aimed the gun that saved our bacon?"

The soldier chuckled. "It was Aaron Schellenger. He'd come along when we moved your gun from here, an' there was nobody else around who'd ever fired a cannon. Aaron said he aimed at her waterline, an' the shot went high. It was pure luck he hit anything at all. The ball carried her topmast away."

Will had joined his father on the afterdeck, and he laughed when he heard about Aaron's shooting. "Have to remember to make him a gunner's mate, Dad," he said, "if we go on another voyage, that is."

Not wanting to disturb the household, they slept aboard the sloop and didn't start for home until after breakfast. The wind had shifted easterly, and a steady drizzle was falling as they plodded across the fields.

"Weather's not very good for farmin'," the captain remarked. "Maybe we'd better try another privateerin' trip if we can get our cannon back. This might be a good time, with the British down in the Chesapeake."

Nothing could have pleased Will more than this suggestion. He knew they might find themselves in more tight places—might even be killed in battle. But the excitement of the first cruise was still in his blood, and he yearned for any sort of revenge against an arrogant enemy. Like a million other Americans, he was bitterly angry over what had happened in Washington.

The kitchen at home was warm and snug after their tramp in the rain. Will's mother and sisters were full of questions about the voyage up the Delaware. Faith even wanted to know what the Philadelphia ladies were wearing and seemed amazed that Will hadn't noticed.

His father was just telling them the bad news about the sacking of the nation's Capitol when Roger Thornhill came into the room. His face had a look of shock when he heard what had happened.

"Does that mean the colonies will surrender?" he stammered unhappily.

"No, my boy," said Ezra Hand. "It means we've just begun to fight. An' by the way, we're the United States of America now—not colonies."

"Sorry I used the wrong word again, sir," Roger told him. "But I feel better knowing the war will go on. I suppose I was thinking of what would happen if an enemy captured London. Probably we'd keep on fighting, too."

Will looked at the young prisoner curiously. "You mean," he asked, "you'll be happier if the British don't win?"

Roger's eyes dropped. "Yes," he said in embarrassment. "I know it sounds unpatriotic, but I've come to like this country of yours. Do you know I've been helping a little on the farm?"

"Indeed he has," Martha Hand put in. "He's fed the pigs an' hunted eggs an' brought in the cows at night. He even tried a little milking!"

"Good!" said the captain heartily. "Sounds as if you'd about got over your wound, Roger. Well, we don't have to tell that to the militia. They'd prob'ly want to haul you off to jail."

"Don't you let 'em do that!" Lovey and Faith cried together. And Will felt much the same way. For a Britisher, he thought, Roger was all right.

*   *   *

Preparations for the *Fair Molly's* second venture were delayed for a few days. First, as soon as the rain stopped, Will and his father had to mow and bring in the oats, already overripe. Then Will encountered a little trouble finding Lieutenant Townsend to ask him for the return of the cannon. The militia had moved its camp again. This time they had gone north to Dennis Creek, to guard the shipyard there. It was a ride of close to twenty miles, and it gave Black Prince a good workout.

Josh Townsend was perfectly willing to let them have the long nine once more, but naturally the Hand family would have to transport it.

"Have you caught Ferd Leech spyin' on your troops?" Will asked, and the lieutenant smiled at him.

"We've been sort o' busy," he replied, "what with saving your sloop from that schooner and a few other things. However, I did send a couple o' the boys to watch the tavern. After two days and nights they reported they'd seen nothing suspicious."

Will shook his head in disappointment. "Well," he said, "somebody must've sent a signal that we'd be comin' 'round the point that night. The schooner was just out there waitin' for us."

The lieutenant had to admit that it looked that way. "What we ought to do," he said, "is try to find the new signal place and then catch the man that's using it. Anyhow, there don't seem to be any ships out there now, so you shouldn't have any trouble. When do you want that gun?"

"Maybe tomorrow night," Will told him. "I reckon Dad won't want to haul it in daylight if there's a spy around."

He rode home and gave his father the message. And Captain Hand agreed to go for the cannon the following night.

It was September now, and the evening was chilly when Will helped to harness the old mare to the wagon. Then he put on his pea jacket as he climbed to the seat beside his father. In the last of the daylight, they started northward up the road. There was no lantern on the wagon, and they rode in silence. The last thing Ezra Hand wanted was to attract attention to this trip. He even took a back road so as to avoid passing Leech's Tavern, and Will heartily approved of the maneuver.

They were moving through a patch of woods below the village of Goshen when old Bess lifted her head with a sudden snort. In the moonlight the sandy road lay empty. But off to the right there was a sound of something scurrying away through the brush.

"Deer, most likely," Will's father grunted. "That or a bobcat. Could even be a bear, I s'pose. Giddap, old lady!"

Will was far from convinced that an animal had made the noise, but he said nothing. About midnight they reached the militia camp and were challenged by a sentry. Most of the men were lying in their blankets asleep, but Josh Townsend was alert, as usual. With the help of three or four soldiers, roused by the lieutenant, they hoisted the gun carriage up on the wagon bed and tied it firmly in place. Then, as quietly as they had come, they started the return journey.

"Here, Will, you drive," said the captain. "I'm gettin' too sleepy."

The moon had been hidden by clouds, and it was very dark when Will took the reins. The road was only a shade lighter than the surrounding blackness, and Will made no effort to guide the mare. He knew she could find the way better than he.

After a while it seemed to grow even darker. A drop of rain splashed on Will's face, then another, and soon it was coming down steadily. He hunched down into the collar of his jacket and looked at his father, snoring gently beside him. Rain meant nothing to the veteran skipper.

Will did his best to be equally unmoved by the weather. One thing about it comforted him. Surely no spy was going to endure the discomfort of sneaking about in the wet woods on such a night.

Old Bess plodded on. It was impossible to get her moving faster than a walk, pulling such a load, but even so they should reach Cold Spring by daylight. Actually the rain let up a few miles from home, and a star or two began to appear. The first roosters were challenging each other from farm to farm when Will saw the mare prick up her ears and begin to step faster. She was heading for home.

Will got down and opened the door of the barn when they got there. His father woke and instructed him to lead the mare inside.

141

"Unhitch her an' rub her down," he said. "We'll leave the gun on the wagon till tomorrow night. That'll give us time to round up the crew again. First, though, we'd better get some sleep."

✿　✿　✿

As darkness fell the following night, they carted the cannon down to the dock where the *Fair Molly* was moored. The same group of young men who had sailed with them earlier had assembled aboard the schooner, and they quickly moved the nine-pounder from the wagon to the deck. Will greeted them all. He was especially glad to see Aaron Schellenger.

"They tell me you can do more with the old cannon than just lug it around," he told the big young fisherman. "Good thing you happened to be on hand that night we started up the bay!"

"I ain't braggin' about that," Aaron answered. "My aim was pretty bad."

"Well," the captain put in, "it was good enough to save our skins, an' we're mighty grateful. All right, boys, bring your seabags aboard an' let's go."

Hannibal had laid in more supplies while the sloop was at the dock, and he assured the skipper that they had food and water for a week's cruise, at least. About eleven o'clock that night, all was ready to cast off. They sailed out of Cold Spring Inlet and headed up the coast, close-hauled against a northeast wind.

Still short of sleep, Will took the first watch below. He was roused out at four in the morning and sent aloft to replace Jonathan Jenkins at the masthead. The coast, as he well knew, was just a long succession of beaches and dunes, but he did recognize the rugged entrance to Townsend's Inlet as they beat past it. A few moments later, as they tacked nearer to shore, he made out a flickering light on the beach. He waited till he was sure, then hailed the deck.

"Somebody's built a fire there to port," he told the helmsman. "Looks like a bonfire on the beach."

Amos Stilwell was at the tiller. He called Matt Hughes to take it and hurried up the ratlines with the spyglass.

He confirmed Will's guess. "There's men around the fire an' a boat pulled up on the sand. If we were near enough to smell what they're cookin', I'd lay a wager it'd be fresh-killed beef. I'm goin' to call the cap'n."

In a minute or two Ezra Hand was up there with Will. "Where'd the boat come from?" he asked his son gruffly. "You been so busy watchin' the fire you didn't bother to look anywhere else? There's a ship off here somewhere, an'—there—I see her. A snow, I'd judge, right abeam to starboard!"

He climbed down and brought the sloop into the wind while he counseled with the mate. Then he gave his orders.

"Get your gun ready, Hannibal. The rest o' you, grab your muskets. We'll tackle the snow first. If the boat's hers, she'll be shorthanded. Will, run up our colors."

He brought the *Fair Molly* over to leeward, and she picked up speed with the wind abeam. Will had descended now and picked up his loaded musket. The snow was a squatty vessel with two short masts and square sails. Her type was ordinarily used for cargo in coastal waters, and she was a sluggish sailer.

As soon as her lookout sighted the big sloop bearing down upon her, she swung off to sea in a vain attempt to run away. Within a mile Captain Hand brought the *Fair Molly* alongside in hailing distance.

"What ship is that?" he bellowed. "Heave to or we'll sink you!"

A quavering voice replied that she was the *Gretchen*, out of Perth Amboy.

"Collectin' beef to feed the British fleet, I'll warrant!" growled the skipper. "Heave to, like I told you. We're comin' aboard. An' no false moves or my gunners'll blow you out o' water!"

The sea was calm enough to lower the boat, and in a matter of minutes Captain Hand and three sailors had boarded the other craft. As soon as the surrender was completed, the boat returned for the mate, and Will and Hannibal were left to handle the sloop. Then his father, with Schellenger and Hughes, came back aboard.

"Just as I figured," the captain said. "Her hold's full o' fresh beef, killed along the shore. Her skipper says there are three men over on the beach. If that's all there are, we can take 'em prisoner without much of a fight."

"You didn't have any trouble with the snow?" asked Will.

"Nope. Her cap'n's a Dutchman, tryin' to make money out o' the war. Only had one other hand aboard, an' they're both in irons now."

While he spoke, he was bringing the sloop about for the run to the beach. Will knew it was the custom of the main-

144

land farmers to turn some of their cattle loose on the coastal islands, where they ran wild all summer. They were a tempting prize for pirates, smugglers, enemy ships, and others who wanted meat.

As they neared the shore, the sun was rising out of the sea astern. The fire was still smoldering, but they could see men hastily throwing beef carcasses into the boat and trying to shove off. They were hardly in the surf when the sloop hove to a hundred yards offshore.

Captain Hand picked up the speaking trumpet. "I've got a nine-pounder ready to sink you!" he roared. "Pull back to the beach!"

At once he sent Aaron, Matt, and Will off in the sloop's boat. "Don't expect they'll give you trouble," he said, "but bring 'em back anyhow, with the boat an' the beef."

Will and Matt were at the oars, and Aaron Schellenger sat in the stern with a loaded rifle across his knees. As they got into the swells near shore, the boat heaved high, then dropped into the trough, but the two rowers were good enough seamen to keep her from broaching to. They caught the curling crest of the next wave and were driven toward the beach at breathtaking speed. And just as the bow scraped the sand, a gunshot rang out.

The bullet splintered the boat's gunwale, halfway between the rowers, and Will turned hastily to see who had fired.

The boat rested firmly on the beach now, and Aaron was standing up, tall and formidable.

"Drop that gun!" he barked. "The first one that tries to fire is a dead man!"

Fourteen

Sullenly, two of the men on the beach threw down their muskets. The third one was unarmed.

"Matt," said Aaron, "go pick up their guns an' bring 'em here."

When it was done, he ordered the cattle killers back into their boat and, still covering them with the rifle, told them to row out to the sloop. As soon as he saw them being hauled aboard, he helped the other two boys load several sides of beef into their own craft. Matt had taken a quick look at the pile of hides.

"That's one o' my father's cows!" he exclaimed. "I can tell by the earmarks. The others are Townsend cattle."

"Well, these fellows'll go to jail for it," Aaron told him. "You'd better just thank your stars that bullet missed you."

They launched their boat through the surf and followed

the prisoners back to the *Fair Molly*. That day the crew dined well on steaks that Hannibal fried. And meanwhile, the sloop and her prize were sailing on up the coast. Early in the afternoon they entered Great Egg Inlet. The *Gretchen* came lumbering along behind them, and before dusk they had tied up at the dock in Beesley's Point.

Will looked around for their former prize, the schooner *Lady Gay*, but she was nowhere to be seen. It was a month since they had brought her in, and he hoped her absence meant she had been sold. A short time later a militia officer came to greet Ezra Hand and told them the schooner had been auctioned off a week before.

"She's up at May's Landing now," he said. "Going to be fitted out as a privateer, so I've heard. She was staunch enough an' had good lines, so I guess she brought a fair price. The Committee o' Safety has your prize money. No cargo, so it won't be much, but better'n nothing."

Captain Hand chuckled. "Wait till you see what we brought in this time," he said. "Wild beef off the islands! And a clumsy old snow that can't be worth more'n a few dollars. Hope you've got room for a new bunch o' prisoners."

"We won't keep 'em long," the militiamen answered. "If they're cattle thieves, they belong in the county jail, down at Middle Town."

Both Will and his friend Matt were too tired to have any thoughts of calling on girls that night. They turned in as soon as they were off duty and slept like logs till morning.

Shortly after breakfast Will's father went off to see the clerk of the Upper Township Committee of Safety, and when he came back to the sloop, he went into the cabin to work out the shares. Each ordinary member of the crew received thirty-five dollars of prize money from the sale of the *Lady Gay*. It wasn't a fortune, but it was more money than any of the young men could earn in a month at home, and they all felt rich.

That afternoon Hannibal went ashore to buy fresh eggs and vegetables. And as soon as he returned, Captain Hand told the crew to get ready for departure. As darkness fell, they sailed out into the bay and headed for the inlet.

None of them expected to encounter any ships that night, but hardly were they outside when Jonathan Jenkins, at the masthead, reported sails to the east and south. The moon came through the clouds then, and even the men on deck could see its light on the upper canvas of a whole fleet of vessels—at least a dozen that Will could count.

"Must be a convoy," his father conjectured. "Looks like two men-o-war are herdin' 'em along. We'll stay close inshore till they get past."

The convoy ships were of all sizes, from small brigs to full-rigged merchant vessels. The two frigates guarding them were faster than any of the cargo ships, and after making what seemed to be an effort to hurry the laggards along, they sailed north to take stations at the head of the fleet.

"Amos," said the captain to his mate, "are you thinkin' what I am?"

Stilwell nodded. "That brig at the tail end o' the line

looks to be droppin' farther behind," he said. "If we're lucky, maybe we could cut her out."

"Right!" the skipper told him. "Soon as that big cloud covers the moon, we'll go after her."

The wind was out of the southeast and favored their chase. It was soon so dark that the lookout could barely see the brig, now a mile or so ahead. But the *Fair Molly*, with every sitch of canvas drawing, gained on her rapidly.

The captain went aloft with his glass to get a better view if possible, and when he returned to the deck, he rubbed his hands.

"She's yawin' a lot," he told the mate. "That may be one reason she's so slow. Looks to me like the steersman must be drunk. I couldn't make out any gunports, so I doubt if she's armed."

As they pulled closer, Will could see two men running to trim the yards. They must have sighted the sloop and were trying to get more speed out of their square sails. Hannibal came aft to speak to the skipper.

"Gun's loaded, sir," he said. "You want me to give her a warnin' shot?"

"No," was the answer. "Any gunfire'll bring those frigates down on us. I want to take her quiet—an' fast!"

He sailed past to leeward, two hundred feet from the merchantman.

"Ahoy, the brig!" he called. "I've got a long nine trained on your waterline. Heave to—an' quick—or you'll be hulled!"

A drunken laugh came from across the water. "That li'l' ol' boat givin' me orders? Haw, haw!"

Captain Hand swung the tiller over. "Get grapplin' hooks ready!" he commanded. "I'm goin' to board her."

The sea was fairly calm along the side of the brig, and in no time at all the sloop was only yards away. The mate and Aaron Schellenger threw their hooks at the same time, then hauled quickly to bring the vessels together.

"Will—stay at the helm," his father ordered. "Come on, all the rest o' you—up the side!"

Will was bitterly disappointed to be left behind, but he followed instructions. From where he stood at the tiller, he could hear and see all that happened. The privateer's seamen were up and over the rail in a matter of seconds. In the brig's waist, not a hand was raised to stop them. Then the captain of the larger ship came stumbling to the break of the poop, waving a pistol. As Ezra Hand sprang toward him, there was a flash and a bang, but the shot went wild. The Yankee skipper swung himself up to the afterdeck, hit the captain once with his fist, and stood over him as he fell and lay there blubbering.

The rest of the *Fair Molly*'s men had little trouble in overpowering the brig's crew. There were only five hands on deck, and all of them appeared to have been drinking. One big fellow blustered a bit, but Hannibal laid him out with a belaying pin. After that the brig was theirs.

"All right, boys," said Captain Hand crisply, "there's no time to lose. Put 'em in irons an' shove 'em belowdecks. Hannibal, come with me and we'll see who's left."

By the time the prisoners were taken care of, the skipper and his gunner reappeared, pushing three more seamen ahead of them.

"Now," barked the captain, "we'll put these prisoners in the hold o' the sloop. You, Amos, will have Schellenger an' Will to help you sail this craft. Get her turned around an' head for the Great Egg, fast as you can make it. I don't think that pistol shot could be heard aboard the frigates, but you can lay to it that one of 'em's comin' back here soon as they see where the brig is. We'll cover you best we can."

It was Will's first experience in a square-rigged vessel, but he eagerly lent a hand at the halyards, and the sails were soon squared around. The run for the inlet would be a reach with the wind almost abeam.

"She handles like a hay wagon," Stilwell grumbled. "Must have a terrible foul bottom, an' there's somethin' wrong with the rudder."

They had about four miles to go if they were to make the shelter of the inlet. After ten minutes had passed, Will began to breathe easier, for they had surely sailed more than a mile. Then, far astern, they heard the dull, heavy boom of a cannon.

"Come on, old lady!" growled the mate. "Pick up your skirts an' run!"

"Maybe that was just a warning gun to the ships to close up," Aaron suggested. But Will knew it was wishful thinking.

"Moon's out bright now," called Stilwell at the wheel. "Get up aloft, Will, an' see how close they are."

He went cautiously up the old, sagging ratlines, wondering if they would hold his weight. At the main crosstrees he looked northward and saw the clustered topsails of the convoy. Off to windward was another sail, whiter and closer-trimmed. That, he knew, was a frigate, coming south at top speed.

"Sail ho!" he called down. "She's still hull down—I'd say three miles off."

The sloop had circled back and was now within hailing distance. "Did you sight that frigate?" asked Captain Hand. "What's the trouble? Is that all the speed you can get out o' the old tub?"

"We're doin' our best," the mate assured him grumpily. "How much further to the inlet?"

"Only a couple o' miles. But you'll be in range o' the Britisher's guns in another few minutes. Reckon we'd better go an' try to draw her off!"

Looking down from his high perch at the little sloop, Will felt his heart sink. She was so small—so vulnerable, with her single cannon. Yet there she went, sailing valiantly north to meet a ship of at least thirty-six guns and far more speed, smartly handled by a Navy crew. It seemed to be a hopeless task his father had undertaken.

"Will!" barked the mate. "Quit gawkin' up there an' come down an' help with the sails!"

Still looking over his shoulder, Will came down. There was little that he and Aaron could do, but they tried, and the old brig seemed to move a little faster. When he had a chance to look again, the sloop was far to the north of them. Then they heard a big gun fire. The moonlight was bright on the sea, but at that distance it was impossible to tell whether the *Fair Molly* had been hit. After a moment Will saw her sails flutter as she came about. Then they filled again, and she was scudding westward toward the coast.

"No kind of inlet there, is there?" asked Aaron in astonishment. "She'll pile up on the beach!"

But Will had more faith in his father's seamanship. "Just keep watchin'," he said through gritted teeth.

The cannon roared again, and this time they saw a huge spout of white spray not far from the privateer's stern. What was more important was that the frigate had changed course. They had a broadside view of her three masts as she fell off to run before the wind, chasing the smaller vessel.

"It worked!" cried the mate. "Ezra's bought us a few more minutes o' time!"

The entrance to Great Egg Inlet was in clear sight now, just off the brig's starboard bow. At Stilwell's order the boys slacked sheets, and he spun the wheel to bring the wind astern. Clumsily the heavy craft made for the gap like a cow heading for the barn.

When Will found time to look, the point at the lower end of Absecon Island hid the sloop and the pursuing frigate from his view. All he could do now was pray.

Once more a cloud obscured the moon, so that they seemed to be plunging into a void of darkness. Off on either beam there was a faint line of white beach as they sailed through into Great Egg Bay, and Will remembered the sandy islands that blocked the entrance on each side. But the mate knew those waters, and he steered safely between them.

Astern and a little to the north, the frigate's guns roared

154

again and Will shivered. It seemed impossible that shots at that range could miss the *Fair Molly*. With a heavy heart he turned back to his work at the sheet ropes.

"Well," said Aaron, "we're safe enough now. No ship-o'-war is goin' to try to navigate the Great Egg at night. An' don't get upset about the sloop. Could be your dad gave 'em the slip in the dark."

Will didn't attempt to answer. All he could do was cling to the slim hope that Aaron was right.

About four o'clock in the morning, they hove to near the mouth of the Tuckahoe and waited for daybreak. Then, as the sun rose, Amos Stilwell found an American flag in the locker and had it run up to the maintop.

"Don't want any o' those militia batteries firin' on us," he told his little crew.

Slowly they worked the brig in to a mooring alongside the dock and, under the mate's supervision, furled her sails. As soon as they had made themselves known to the guards, Stilwell took Will with him to the cabin. It was dirty and unkempt, but after a few minutes' search they located the brig's papers. The mate took one look at the cargo manifest and whistled under his breath.

"My boy," he said, "we've got ourselves a prize! The hold's full o' rum and Madeira wine! Reckon it's no wonder the officers an' crew were all drunk!"

He went ashore to breakfast at the inn and make his report to the Committee of Safety. Meanwhile, Aaron and Will managed to find some hardtack and a little coffee, which they brewed in the galley. Neither of them had slept at all the night before, and they took turns napping on the deck. It was a little past noon when the mate returned, and he seemed to be in extra good humor.

"They've had some big news from the South," he told the boys. "The British got licked good an' proper when they tried to capture Baltimore! They shelled Fort McHenry most o' the night, but the garrison fought right back an' hulled a couple o' their ships. The word now is that they're pullin' out o' the Chesapeake."

When Stilwell had started to speak, Will thought the good news would be about the *Fair Molly*, and now his spirits sank again. Even if the British had been beaten, his thoughts were centered on the fate of his father and the sloop.

The mate gave each of them twenty-five cents and sent them off to dine at the tavern, which stood near the ferry landing at the north end of the village. The ferry made two trips a day to Somers Point, across the bay. It was a scowlike vessel with four rowers and a single square sail, used only when the wind was right. It was big enough to hold a wagon, though most of the traffic was made up of horses and their riders. The bay at that spot was only a mile and a half across, and the ferry saved a lot of distance for travelers going up to Egg Harbor City, Batsto, or the towns along the Mullica.

Will and Aaron dined well on roast beef, potatoes, and apple pie, then went down to the ferry slip to watch the boat loading for its afternoon trip.

Suddenly Will saw something out of the corner of his eye. Off to the northwest there was a sail—a single-masted vessel bowling along before the wind. Something was wrong with her mainsail, but flying proudly from the top-mast was a tattered flag of red, white, and blue. Will grabbed his friend's arm and pointed, not trusting his voice.

"What did I tell you?" cried Aaron. "That's the *Fair Molly*, sure as a gun's iron!"

Fifteen

They ran all the way to the dock where the brig lay. They were too short of breath to be coherent, but when they gestured toward the bay, Amos Stilwell saw why they were so excited.

"Well, by golly!" he exclaimed. "How she made it I'm durned if I know, but here comes our privateer!"

Will scampered up the ratlines for a better view of the sloop. He could see that her canvas had taken more than one shot, and some of her cordage was hanging loose, but she seemed to be footing about as fast as ever. Soon she was close enough to make out the shapes of men on deck, and he waved with all his might. The figure at the helm could be nobody but his father.

The reunion of the two crews on the dock was a joyful affair. They hugged each other, laughing like children. At

158

last the celebration quieted down enough for questions to be asked.

"So you brought in the prize," said Ezra Hand. "Did she have a decent cargo? What do you figure she's worth?"

"The folks ashore say thirty thousand dollars," Amos told him. "I think it might run more. She's carryin' better'n a hundred hogsheads o' rum an' Madeira. But what we want to know is how you got away!"

"No great trick," the captain replied. "We were under fire an' catchin' it pretty heavy, but that cloud came over the moon an' gave us a chance. I just cut in sharp around the point an' headed north into the back channel. Some of it's shoal water, but we could make it all right with the centerboard up. 'Course, I hoped the frigate would try to follow us, but her cap'n had more sense. We waited back o' the dune till daylight an' then had to repair some riggin' before we came down here."

He turned the prisoners over to the militia and then went to talk with the Safety Committee. When he returned, toward sundown, he made his own examination of the brig. She was the *Queen Anne,* out of Trinidad, and her cargo matched the manifest except that one hogshead of rum was more than half empty.

"It's a wonder her crew made it this far," Captain Hand commented. "Every soul aboard was three-quarters drunk when we captured her. One thing she'll need before the auction is a good swabbin' down. First job tomorrow mornin'll be for you boys to go to work on her."

Will was well rested after sleeping in his own bunk, and he joined the rest of the crew on the *Queen Anne* right after an early breakfast. They scrubbed out the cabin and forecastle and holystoned the deck. When they finished, the old brig was still far from handsome, but at least she was no longer filthy.

They were all tired that night, but it was the captain's decision that they should start home to Cape May.

"Way I figure," he said, "the British fleet that got licked in the Chesapeake'll do one o' two things. Either they'll go on south to attack Mobile or New Orleans, or they'll head back to the Delaware. I want to make Cold Spring Inlet before we find ourselves in the midst of 'em. I'm not worried about that frigate that chased us. She's had to go on with the convoy."

A northeast wind was blowing when they beat their way out of Great Egg Inlet, and heavy clouds covered the moon. All the signs indicated they were in for a September storm—not a hurricane but plenty of rain and wind. So the sloop ran southward under all the canvas she could carry, and Will, shivering in the crosstrees, thought she must be logging more than ten sea miles an hour.

The rain began to lash the sloop as she drove past Townsend's Inlet. In the pitch darkness of the stormy night, it was next to impossible to see anything a mile away. But he did catch the sound of roaring surf on the inlet bar and thought he could make out a white patch of surf there to starboard. He wondered if an approaching sail would be as hard to spot.

However, that thought didn't worry him much. He was certain no other vessel would be able to see the sloop unless she was practically on top of it. Another stretch of time went by, and again Will saw a faint gleam of breakers, probably marking Hereford Inlet. That meant they would be in home waters in less than an hour. Yet for some reason an uneasy feeling kept gnawing at the back of his mind.

His father, down at the helm, could see even less than he, but he brought the sloop in through the Cold Spring Inlet bar as neatly as if it had been daylight. If anything, the wind and rain were increasing in violence. When Will came down from his lookout station, he was wet to the skin and shaking with the cold. He had a mug of steaming coffee, then went to the captain.

"Dad," he said, "I want to go to the farm."

"Better wait till daylight," his father told him. "You can turn in right now an' get the chill out o' your bones."

Will shook his head. His voice held a note of desperation when he answered. "Please, Dad, let me go now. Ma ought to be told we're back safe. You know how she worries."

"All right, if you aren't wet enough already. Tell 'em I'll be along home in the forenoon."

Will thanked him, buttoned his reefer jacket high around his chin, and set off through the rain and the dark. When he stumbled into the dooryard half an hour later, he saw with a shock that there was a light in the kitchen. His premonition that something was wrong hit him harder than ever. Before he reached for the latch, he heard voices inside—one of the girls sobbing and his mother trying to comfort her.

The door was bolted. He shook the latch and called

out, telling them who he was. Martha Hand came to open it, and he saw the trouble in her face.

"What is it, Ma?" he asked with a shiver. "What's happened here?"

She clasped him in her arms. "Tell me, Willing," she said, "is your father safe, too?"

"He's fine," Will assured her. "But something's wrong here. What are you all up for this time o' night?"

"It's Roger," she told him. "Two men came about an hour ago and pounded on the door. They said they were militia and had orders to take him off to jail. But, Will, they didn't sound like Cape May boys to me—more like Englishmen. Roger looked hard at them and refused to go. But they grabbed him and carried him off! We don't know what to do!"

For a moment Will was speechless. Then he put on his rain-soaked hat again and went to the door.

"Dad'll be here in the mornin'," he told his mother. "All o' you try to get some sleep. I'm goin' to go to the militia an' find out if they had anything to do with this."

As he rode northward on the black colt, he had time to think over what he had been told. And the more he thought, the clearer it seemed to him that no militia officers would have ordered the young prisoner removed at three o'clock in the morning. Everything about it smelled wrong. He clucked to Prince, and the eager young horse responded with a faster gallop.

It was still raining when he reached Dennis Creek, but what should have been dawn was beginning to lighten the east. The militia encampment was still there, and the

men were asleep in their sodden tents. One canvas shelter looked a little larger than the others. Will dismounted and went to the flap.

"You there, Josh?" he asked in a low voice. "Lieutenant —are you there?"

There was a grunt from inside. Then Josh Townsend appeared, rubbing the sleep from his eyes.

"Yes," he said gruffly. "What is it?"

Will told him the story as briefly as he could. "My mother thought the two soldiers didn't talk like our folks," he added. "More like Englishmen, she said."

Townsend was fully awake now. "None of our men did it," he told Will flatly. "They must have come ashore somewhere in the southern part of the county, down close to your place. We watch for landings, but maybe they used a small skiff that would be hard to spot in the dark and rain. Sounds to me as if they'd been tipped off that you menfolks were away. I reckon it was that spy again!"

"Then I guess you haven't caught him yet," said Will unhappily.

The lieutenant shook his head. "Have to try a little harder, it looks like."

"Well," said Will, "Roger wasn't to blame. They had to drag him out. I reckon he's back aboard his ship by now."

"What's your father think about it?" asked Townsend.

"He doesn't know it happened. Dad stayed with the sloop when we came in two or three hours ago."

"Have a good voyage?"

"Yes—a lucky one. But this sort o' takes the fun out of it."

"I'll send a squad of men to watch Leech's Tavern if you're convinced they're mixed up in it."

"No," Will told him. "A squad's too many. You pick one good man an' let me go with him, an' we'll stop this spyin' business."

Lieutenant Townsend frowned as he thought it over. Then he nodded. "All right. A man'll drop in at your house this afternoon."

They shook hands, and Will felt a little better as he rode southward again. It wouldn't bring back the kidnaped prisoner, but at least he would feel he was doing something for the Yankee cause. He deliberately avoided passing Leech's Tavern, for he thought the less they knew about his movements, the better.

When he reached home, the storm had blown itself out and the sky was clearing. Tired and wet, he rode to the barn and stabled the colt. Then, as he went toward the house, he saw his father staring at him.

"Thought you'd be snug in bed," said Ezra Hand. "What takes you gallivantin' around the country?"

"You'd better come in an' let Ma tell you," Will answered.

When the full story had been unfolded, the captain sat in the kitchen, stony-faced. "You're sure Roger wasn't in on the scheme?" he asked finally.

"Ezra Hand," said his wife, "sometimes I think men are all born stupid. You believe the girls an' I would be fooled? Why, if he'd been stronger after his wound, he'd have fought 'em. He'd given his word not to escape, an' that meant a lot to the boy!"

The captain nodded. "That's true," he admitted. "So it comes down to how they knew Will an' I'd be away from home. Somebody must ha' seen us sail out an' got word to the British."

They did the morning chores, ate breakfast, and at last

Will was able to catch a few hours of sleep. He got up at noon and was ready to greet the young soldier in homespun who rode into the yard. It was his cousin, Abel Hand. Will was glad his father had gone back to the sloop, for it saved some difficulty in explaining. He simply told his mother that he and Abel had to do an errand for Lieutenant Townsend. They had some dinner, and then he saddled Prince. They rode off together.

"You bring any grub?" his cousin asked. "We may be out a spell, so we'd better stop at my place an' pack a few vittles. Now tell me what we're s'posed to do."

Will gave him what little evidence he had against the Leech family. "If I'm right," he said, "young Ferd has been watchin' our sloop an' findin' out where the militia's quartered. Then somehow he sends messages to the fleet. Dad an' I are sure it was a couple o' British marines that took away Roger Thornhill last night, an' how did they know where to find him if some spy didn't tell 'em? We know just about every family 'round here, an' who else but the Leeches would do such a thing?"

They rode over to the bay shore and along the bluffs for a mile or two. Will wanted to look again at the place where the signal light had been used. But they found no fresh clues there, and after a few minutes' search they went on. Every mile or so they encountered a lone sentry, sitting in the brush or the high grass, where he could command a view of the shore and the creeks.

The bay was no longer empty. Once more, Will saw, a number of ships lay offshore, and he pointed them out to Abel.

"That's right," his companion said. "They've been back

here two or three days now. That big seventy-four out yonder is the *Poictiers,* they say—Commodore Beresford's flagship."

When they came to the Fishing Creek marshes, they turned their horses inland. "You know where Leech's Tavern is," said Will. "It's just down the road a piece from Fishing Creek village. My idea is to wait till near dark an' then get close to it through the woods—not along the road. Then if Ferd goes out to signal the enemy, I can follow him."

It was nearing six o'clock, and they were both hungry. They found a little cleared space in the woods, back from the marsh, where they dismounted and ate some of the food they had brought from Abel's house. The one thing they needed was something to drink, but Will didn't think it was wise to show themselves by getting fresh water at a farm well.

At sunset they rode on westward till the road was almost in sight through the trees. The inn was hidden by a thick grove of cedars, but Will knew it was only a short distance away.

"Look, Abel," he told his cousin, "you'd better stay here with the horses an' keep 'em quiet. I'll go on an' scout around the place. Maybe I won't find anything suspicious, but I've got to try."

Both of them had brought guns, but after thinking it over, Will left his rifle behind with Abel. It would just be in his way if he had to do any crawling. He waited till it grew a little darker, then set off, light-footed, through the woods.

In a short time, he could smell frying bacon and hear a

faint sound of voices, so he was sure the tavern was directly ahead. His heart beat faster as he crouched in the cedar thicket. He heard a door open and close. Then someone with a heavy tread crossed the inn yard, heading toward the stable. From inside it a horse snorted. Perhaps, he thought, there was a stage due shortly, and the man was preparing to bring out a fresh team.

No Indian could have advanced more silently than Will as he approached the rear of the stable, then worked his way around it to the side away from the tavern. There was a pile of earth and brush there, and he hid behind it, watching to see if the man would come out. A sound of jingling harness reached his ears, and a man's rough voice, ordering a horse to stand still.

Suddenly a small dog came yapping across the yard, heading straight for Will's hiding place. He grabbed a stick, but realized that any attempt to drive the dog off would surely draw attention to himself. So, as the animal came closer, he smiled and snapped his fingers, trying to act friendly.

For a moment he thought his strategy had worked. The dog stopped its racket and bounded into the brush pile, its tail wagging. But then came another sound. A different voice called from the direction of the tavern.

"Hey, Tige," it called. "What you got there—a rabbit? Sic 'em, boy!"

Hastily Will tried to back away, but the movement brought a fresh chorus of barks from the little dog. In a panic now, he got to his feet and started to run.

"Hold on, you!" shouted the man who had called to the dog. "Ben—Ferd—come catch this feller!"

The cedar thicket was close. Racing to reach its cover, Will tripped over an arching root and fell headlong on his face. And even as he struggled to get up, something struck him on the back of the head. He was unconscious before he hit the ground.

Sixteen

"You got those knots tight?" growled someone Will couldn't see. "All right, toss him down below with the other one."

Powerful hands seized him under the armpits and dragged him a few feet to an open trapdoor. He was bound and helpless, and he wondered how far he would fall. Actually it wasn't too bad, for the man let him down through the trap before dropping him. He landed on his back, on what seemed to be the dirt floor of a cellar. Then the trapdoor closed, and he was in utter blackness.

He lay there trying to recover his faculties and listened to the tramp of feet overhead. When it stopped, the silence was oppressive. Then he heard a sound of breathing close by.

"Anybody here?" he managed to ask through stiff lips.

"Aye," said a voice. "It's Roger. Is that you, Will?"

"Roger!" he gasped. "I thought you'd be back aboard your ship 'fore this! What are you doin' here?"

"Sh!" said Roger. "We'd better speak low. The men who came for me last night were marines off the *Poictiers*. They couldn't go back to the ship in daylight, so they brought me here to wait for darkness. Are you hurt, Will?"

"Got a big lump on the back o' my skull an' a mean headache, that's all. I was pretty stupid to get caught, but I've suspected these tavern folks for quite a while, an' I came to scout the place."

"Is that where we are?" asked the English boy. "I was blindfolded when they dragged me in here."

"Gosh!" Will groaned. "I wonder what Abel's goin' to think when I don't come back. He's my cousin, an' I left him back o' the woods with our horses. If he knew, I reckon he'd go an' bring the militia. But he'll wait for a spell, an' by then it'll be too late."

"Will," said the young midshipman, "you don't think I broke my parole, do you? I wouldn't have done that for anything."

"Shucks, no! My mother an' the girls told me how it was, an' it sure wasn't your fault. Listen—they're stirrin' 'round up there!"

"Is it dark yet?" Roger asked. "I've been here so long, I've no idea of time."

"Yep. Dark enough. They'll likely come an' get us pretty quick."

Hardly had he spoken when the trapdoor was flung open and light shone faintly into the cellar. Then a big man let himself down. He had a lantern in his hand.

When he had hung it on a nail in one of the supporting beams, he seized Roger and carried him to the trap. As he lifted the boy up, arms reached down through the opening and hoisted him the rest of the way.

Then Will was treated in the same fashion. After he was dumped on the sanded floor, he could see four men in the bar. One, the youngest, had a shock of black hair and a mean, foxlike face. Will had no doubt that he was Ferd Leech. And another, who resembled him but had a bald head fringed with gray, must be Ichabod Leech, his father. The other two were stocky and broad-shouldered, with the stolid, weather-tanned faces of British marines.

"No light, now," one of them ordered. "We'll bring the prisoners. And you, young Leech, go in front to see there's nobody about."

They took off the ropes that bound Will's feet but left his wrists still tied behind him. Roger's legs were already freed. Then they were pushed roughly out the door into the autumn night. Both of them had been gagged.

"No grunts out o' you, chappie," one of the men whispered in Will's ear. "Just remember this knife'll be in your ribs if there's a false move."

They went quietly up the road, staying in the shadow of the woods. After something less than half a mile, Ferd turned off suddenly to the left. The marines stopped their two prisoners and waited for him to scout the woods ahead. Then they heard a whippoorwill's call that must have been Leech's signal.

Will was shoved into the brush and went stumbling along in the direction from which the whistle had come.

172

After a short distance his feet sank into wet muck, and he realized he was in the edge of the marsh. Nobody spoke, but the two boys were prodded on till they came to the bank of a narrow creek.

"All safe, is it?" asked one of the marines in a low voice.

"Yeah," Ferd Leech whispered. "You'll be all right till you get to the bay. An' it oughta be pitch-dark by then. How 'bout my pay?"

"We paid your father," the marine growled. "Get on 'ome with you, now."

Young Leech started to whine for more money, but he was quickly silenced.

"Want the 'ole Yankee militia down on us?" snapped the Englishman. "You keep your trap shut!"

A small boat, painted some dark color, lay there in the reeds at the water's edge. Into it the marines pushed Will and Roger, making them lie down under the midships thwart. One of the Britishers took his place in the stern, while the other picked up a pair of oars and sat just forward of the boys. He pushed off and began rowing.

The oars must have been muffled, for there was no sound as the little skiff moved slowly down the waterway. Will was trying to figure where they were, and he decided they must be in the south branch of Fishing Creek.

Fortunately it was too chilly for mosquitoes. The boys, with their hands tied, would have been in agony otherwise. Their captors seemed to be in no hurry. Slowly and quietly the boat glided downstream through the twisting channel, always hidden by tall reeds.

Wild ideas of making an escape whirled through Will's

mind. He thought of making a sudden lunge over the side. Perhaps it would upset the boat, adding to the confusion. Perhaps he could squirm into the bulrushes and hide there. He must have fidgeted with the rope around his wrists, for at that moment the man in the stern poked him in the ribs.

"Just remember, me lad," he muttered. "The knife!"

Will clenched his teeth to stop the tremor of fear that ran through him at those words. All he could do was lie still and wait for another chance.

It must have taken them at least an hour to reach the mouth of Fishing Creek. There were no other boats there and no house within sight. The surface of the bay was calm that night, and the sky was overcast, with only one or two stars showing. Steadily, without any change in his stroke, the rower pulled out into open water.

Will wondered if a guard along the bluffs could see them—a dark dot in the dark expanse. But even if he did, what could he do? With each moment the boat was moving farther from shore. Only a much faster craft could overtake them now. Ten or fifteen minutes went by, and suddenly he blinked his eyes, for there, directly ahead, loomed the bulk of a big ship, her lofty masts reaching upward into the night.

"She's in sight, 'Erb," said the man in the stern. "Just 'old your course steady as you go."

The ship looked bigger and bigger as they drew near. Will could see the white striping of her gunports now— three tiers of them—and he knew she must be the seventy-four-gun *Poictiers*.

The marine facing the two boys shipped his oars, and the little boat bobbed alongside. "Ahoy, there!" called the man in the stern. "Drop us a ladder. We've got prisoners."

In a moment Will, his hands freed, was climbing up the rope ladder with the knife-wielding marine right behind him. Roger followed, and the other marine took only time to make the falls fast to the boat. It was hoisted up almost as soon as Will reached the top. Lanterns lit up the deck.

A stiff-looking Navy lieutenant acknowledged the marines' salute and stared at the prisoners with his nose in the air. "Midshipman Thornhill, is it?" he said in a clipped British accent. "You'll be dealt with later, Thornhill. But who's this country bumpkin? One of their militiamen, no doubt."

"No, sir, beggin' your pardon, sir," answered one of the marines. " 'E's off a privateer, sir—the one we've 'ad trouble with, I'm told."

"Ha!" snorted the officer. "Put them both in the brig for the moment. I'm sure the commodore will want to question them."

The two were hustled forward and down a ladder into the ship's brig. It was a stuffy little compartment, about six feet by ten, and with such scant headroom that neither boy could stand straight. The heavy door clanged shut behind them, and they heard a bolt being shot home. There was one stool and one straw pallet in the place, and the only light came from a barred skylight overhead.

"Well," said Roger. "Here we are! I wonder what they plan to do with us."

"Shucks!" Will replied with more assurance than he felt. "You'll come off all right—prob'ly be returned to duty 'fore you know it. Me—I don't know. I guess I'm a prisoner o' war. Hope they give us some water soon. I'm mighty dry."

The lights began to go out above. "You take the cot," said Will. "I'm used to sleepin' on the bare deck."

The night seemed endless to both of them, for they had plenty of things to worry about. But at least, Will thought, he could stand it better as long as he had Roger for company.

They could hear the ship's bells calling the hours. Will was wakened from a restless sleep about six o'clock in the morning when somebody rattled the bolt on the door. A marine guard came in with two rations of hardtack and a single pannikin of scummy, greenish liquid.

"No more water?" asked Roger. "This lad's thirsty."

"We're short o' water," growled the guard. "Yanks drive off our boats when we try to fill the water butts. So it's your own fault, young laddy-buck!"

When he had put the rations down and locked them in again, Roger handed the pannikin to Will.

"You drink it," he said. "I'm not as thirsty as you. They treated me fairly well at the tavern."

Will shut his eyes and sipped at the unappetizing stuff. It was all he could do to swallow it, but it did quench a little of his thirst.

Two hours later, Roger was taken out for questioning. In spite of his cheerful words to his friend, Will wondered how his case would go. He had heard of the harsh discipline in the British Navy, and he supposed it was possible the young midshipman might be considered a deserter. And the longer Roger was gone, the more despondent he became.

At last, late in the forenoon, the guard reappeared. "Come on, you," he ordered. "Make yourself as decent as you can. You're goin' to the commodore's cabin."

There was little Will could do to help his appearance. His homespun shirt was torn, his dungarees were muddy, and there was no way to wash his face. He did run his fingers through his matted hair. Then he followed the guard aft, blinking in the sunlight, and finally arrived in front of the carved door of the flag officer's quarters.

Commodore John P. Beresford sat behind his great teak table and looked quizzically at the Yankee boy. He was a large man, with a ruddy face and grizzled hair. In his spotless uniform and finely frilled linen, he looked the perfect pattern of a British sea commander. To Will's surprise he was smiling.

"What's your name, lad?" he asked politely.

"Willing Hand, sir, from Cold Spring, in Cape May County."

"Hm, are you a sailor?"

"Partly, sir. An' partly farmer."

"What sort of craft have you sailed in?"

"Just a sloop, sir. She used to be my father's pilot boat."

"And now what is she?"

"Well, sir, she was a packet sailing to Philadelphia up until the blockade. Now my father has a letter of marque."

"Aha, now we're getting there. A privateer, eh?"

"Yes, sir," Will admitted, just above a whisper.

"Have you had some successful cruises?" asked the commodore with a straight face.

"That depends, sir. Yes, we've taken a few small ships."

"And where's your ship now, Mr. Hand?"

"I'm sorry, sir, but I don't think I should say."

178

Beresford nodded as if he had expected the answer. "I dare say you're quite right, my boy," he said. "But of course we're kept informed of these things. By the way, are you acquainted with young Mr. Thornhill?"

"Yes, sir."

"Well acquainted, would you say?"

"Yes, sir. After he was wounded, my mother nursed him at our farm. He gave his promise that he wouldn't try to escape."

Now the commodore frowned. "You're certain of that?" he asked.

"Sure I am, sir. If they'd kept him in the jail, I reckon he never would have gotten well. So Josh—er, the lieutenant—let him come to our place on parole. I know Roger'd rather die than go back on his word."

Something of Will's earnestness must have communicated itself to Commodore Beresford. He nodded his head slowly.

"Thank you," he said. "Guard, take this young man out and quarter him with the other prisoners. Then send Mr. Thornhill in here again."

Will was led forward to a hatch leading to one of the gundecks. From there they descended again till they were in a dark area forward of the orlop deck. Two marines stood guard at an iron-studded door, and when it was opened, Will expected to see another little cage like the brig. Instead it turned out to be a roomy place, some fifty feet long, narrowing into the bow of the ship. There were bunks along the sides, and sitting or lying on them were half a dozen American prisoners.

Enough daylight came in through the small portholes for Will to get a good look at them. They appeared to be well fed and reasonably contented with their lot. After the door had closed, they got up to greet the newcomer.

"Where you from, boy?" asked one lanky fellow in a slow Southern drawl. "You're a Jerseyman, eh? What sort of outfit were you soldierin' with?"

He explained that he was a seaman off a privateer but didn't go into details about his capture. All but one of the men, it turned out, were soldiers from Maryland and Virginia, taken in the Bladensburg fighting. The other one had fallen overboard off a gunboat in Hampton Roads and been fished out of the water by the British.

While Will was getting acquainted, eight bells were sounded for noon. The other prisoners hurried to their bunks to get their bowls and spoons. And almost at once a cook's helper came in with a kettle of soup. Fortunately for Will, he also brought a wooden porringer and a spoon for the new prisoner.

The soup was hot and tasted fairly good, in spite of the water that had been used. "Scouse" was what the men called it. Eaten with hardtack, it made a fairly filling meal. At least there seemed to be no danger of anyone's starving to death.

It wasn't until he had eaten and was lying on his bunk that Will began to think about his people at home. Long before this, Abel must have reported him missing, and his mother would be sitting, pale and silent, certain that her son was dead. The longer he thought of her distress, the more miserable he felt.

180

Unable to stay quiet, he rose and went across to a port-hole that faced toward the New Jersey shore. It was miles away, but he could make out the low, sand-colored bluffs and the crowning green of woods. He swallowed hard to keep back a sob of homesickness and returned slowly to his bunk.

Seventeen

"What's wrong, young 'un?" asked the gunboat sailor. "Somethin' botherin' you?"

Will shook his head. "Just can't help wonderin' what they think at home," he said. "I never told 'em where I was goin'."

"Don't fret about it," one of the other prisoners advised. "Just think how tickled they'll be when you come home all safe an' sound. We all figger it won't be long now 'fore we git exchanged."

Will tried to think of his plight that way, but he knew too well how long such negotiations could drag on. So he turned his thoughts to the activities of the Leech family. Surely Josh Townsend would take steps to wipe out that nest of traitors now that it was certain they had captured him. Even though Abel hadn't been aware of what was happening at the tavern, he knew that was where Will had gone.

But revenge on the Leeches would hardly help him in

his present situation. In the end, he resigned himself to accepting things as they were. He would keep as healthy as he could and wait for whatever might come.

The prisoners were fed again at six. No lamps were provided in their quarters, so it grew quite dark a little after sunset. The bunk Will had chosen had a clean straw mattress and was comfortable enough, so that he slept well. The morning dawned cloudy. Soon after breakfast rain began to fall, and there was general grumbling from the prisoners.

"Sometimes they let us out on deck for a bit if the weather's fair," one of them explained. "It don't give us much exercise, but the fresh air feels good, anyhow."

The words stirred the beginning of an idea in Will's brain. He had measured the portholes and knew they were too small for him to crawl through. But if he were free and out on deck, it seemed to him that he might find some chance to escape. Maybe it was crazy even to think about it, but he couldn't keep his imagination from working. There was his own home county only a couple of miles away, and from all appearances, the *Poictiers* would stay at anchor where she lay for a while. If she should be ordered out to sea, of course, his chances would go glimmering. And for that very reason he wanted to act soon.

The rain kept on all that day while Will sat, dejected. After a time he started pacing up and down the length of the compartment until his fellow prisoners got angry and threatened to tie him in his bunk.

The guard who brought the evening meal tried to cheer Will up. "Me lad," he said, "you don't know 'ow good you've got it 'ere. In the 'ulks now there'd be no room to walk about or even to stand up. Filthy, dirty quarters, too, an' food to turn a man's stomach. You'd better pray the commodore don't take it in 's 'ead to send you there!"

Will had heard of the hulks, of course. They were water-logged old prison ships anchored inside Sandy Hook. A man sent to the hulks, his Yankee friends believed, was likely to starve or die of disease or be eaten by rats. Considering all this, he decided the guard was right. He was lucky to be where he was.

On the other hand, his decision to escape if he could was as firm as ever. Listening as he lay in his bunk that night, he knew the rain had stopped. With that thought to help him, he went to sleep. And when he woke in the morning, a ray of sunshine came through the port.

At last, in the middle of the forenoon, the door was flung open. "All right, you lubbers!" cried the guard cheerfully. "All out on deck for a bit of exercise!"

The orlop deck, lowest of the ship's three gun-decks, was hardly a promenade. Most of the space was filled with the cannon and their tackle. Half a dozen marines lounged about with their musket butts resting on the deck. They were there, Will supposed, to keep watch over the prisoners, and their presence would make his plan more difficult.

The gunports had been thrown open so that sun and air could dry the wet deck. At the same time, the cannon had been hauled back into loading position. The prisoners had to pick their way between the gun carriages as they strolled forward and aft.

This went on for nearly half an hour, and Will's courage sank lower as he realized the exercise period must end soon. Then there was a sudden shrilling of a bosun's pipe and a thud of running feet overhead.

"Call to quarters!" an excited voice shouted from the companionway. "Battle stations, all!"

The marines sprang to attention and started for the ladder on the double. Meanwhile, Will could hear the rapid clank of the capstan as the anchor chain came up, and a confused clamor of orders told him the big ship's sails were being hoisted.

The guard who had let them out now recalled his duty. "Come on, you Yanks—back in your cage!" he ordered.

Obediently the rest of the captives crowded toward the prison door, but Will wasn't among them. There had been an instant in the confusion when nobody was looking, and he had seized the opportunity to dart between two cannon. Now he hid under one of the fat black muzzles.

It was no place to stay, he soon realized. If the *Poictiers* was going into battle, the gun crews would come at any moment. He heard the guard slam the door shut and draw the bolt, and it seemed his absence, so far, had gone unnoticed.

Now, he thought, was the time. Shivering, he crept to the open gunport, drew a deep breath, and looked down at the waves twenty feet below. Then he dived outward, head-first. As soon as he hit the water, he stripped off his shoes and swam back under the overhang of the ship's prow. The choppy seas slapped at him there, but he knew no one could see him from above. So he waited, catching his breath and steeling himself for a long, hard swim.

The water of the bay was even colder than he had expected, but he moved his arms and legs vigorously to shake off the chill. The decision as to when to strike out for shore was quickly taken out of his hands. The great ship-of-war began to move forward. Will felt the slippery hull slide past his body, slowly at first, then faster and faster. He waited until the tall stern surged by, then started to swim.

For several minutes all he thought of was getting as far from the ship as possible. Then he lifted his head and was surprised to see her driving along, a good half mile to the northward. Farther away, he made out the topsails of another ship, and for a brief instant, riding the top of a wave, he saw the flash of red, white, and blue at her peak! An American frigate—possibly the *Wasp!*

It was too difficult to keep his head above the waves, so Will gave up watching and centered all his efforts on getting to shore. Every time he looked in that direction the New Jersey coastline seemed as far away as ever.

But he refused to be discouraged. Swimming on manfully, he thought how wonderful his luck had been so far and resolved that no weakness of his own should spoil it.

After what seemed like hours to his tired body, he looked again at the shore. The bluffs were higher now, and the trees on top were green against the sky. Right in front of him was a little inlet that he thought was Cox Hall Creek.

A cramp in his left leg frightened him for a moment, but he took a deep breath, floated a little while, and found it went away. After that he labored on, each stroke a painful effort, and at last his feet touched bottom!

When Will had dragged himself out on the narrow

beach, he was so grateful that he could have kissed the sand. Far up the bay he heard the roar of cannon and struggled to his feet to stare in that direction. The *Poictiers* was barely in sight, half a dozen miles to the north, and the Yankee ship was out of his view completely.

It was strange, he thought, that the sound of gunfire wasn't repeated. If the two ships were closely engaged, there should have been broadside after broadside. But after that one burst, the engagement seemed to have ended. He hoped with all his heart that the *Wasp*, if it was she, had shown her heels to the big seventy-four.

Stumbling with weariness, he clambered up the bluff and set off across country toward Cold Spring. It must be past noon, for the sun was behind him, in the west. The numbing chill went out of his bare feet before he had walked very far, and the nearness of home seemed to put fresh strength into his muscles.

✿   ✿   ✿

The familiar sight of the dooryard brought a lump in Will's throat. As he limped toward the back door, it was flung open suddenly, and his sister Faith came flying to meet him.

"Will!" she cried. "It's you! Where in the world have you been? We thought you must be—we were scared that you—"

"I know," he said. "You were sure I was dead. Wait till I get a little rest, and I'll tell you how close I came to it. Where's Ma?"

"Right here in the kitchen. She saw you and started to cry."

Will opened the door and did his best to smile. His

mother, too, was smiling through her tears.

"I'm still wet, Ma," he said, "so don't try to hug me. But I'm awful glad to be home!"

"You *are* wet, Willing. You look like a drowned rat! I've told you not to go swimming with your clothes on! And no shoes!"

He couldn't help laughing at her. "Yes, Ma," he said. "I swam half way across Delaware Bay to reach home, an' all I get's a scolding!"

While the girls listened openmouthed, he gave them a brief account of his capture and escape. "Where's Dad?" he asked when he had finished.

"Out trying to find some trace of you," Martha Hand replied. "He hasn't slept in his bed since we heard you were missing."

By the time Will had changed into dry clothes and combed his hair, there was a meal waiting for him in the kitchen. After eating several slices of fresh-baked bread with butter and jam and drinking a whole pitcher of milk, he felt like himself again.

"What happened to Roger?" Lovey asked him, her cheeks reddening.

"He's all right, I reckon. The commodore seemed to believe it, about his bein' on parole, an' I'm pretty sure he's back on duty. Maybe he'll write you a letter," he added teasingly.

Just then there was a sound of hoofs in the yard, and through the window he saw his father ride toward the barn. Will jumped up from the table and hurried out. "Dad," he called, "I'm back!"

Ezra Hand dropped the saddle he had just taken off the

colt's back and stood staring at his son, only half believing his eyes.

When he spoke, it was with his usual gruffness. "Well, Will, you sure managed to give us a scare. Where you been, anyhow?"

Once more he told his story, this time in greater detail. "I hope those Leeches are in jail by now," he said. "Did the militia arrest 'em?"

His father's face clouded, and he shook his head. "Josh Townsend took a squad over to question 'em," he said, "but there was nobody home. All Abel could tell the militia was that he waited a long time an' you didn't come back. Said he heard a dog bark a few times, but that was all. So Josh figured he didn't have enough evidence. He went to the tavern again an' found Ichabod there alone. Leech acted as surprised as anybody when he heard you were missin', but said he hadn't seen you an' couldn't help. When Josh asked him where Ferd was, he told him his son had taken the stage to the city a couple o' days before. So that's about where things stand now."

Will ground his teeth together in rage. "Just my word against theirs won't be enough, I s'pose," he muttered. "Josh'll lean over backward to be fair. But I'm goin' to catch those traitors yet!"

"You better stay clear of 'em right now," his father told him sternly. "Let me do the scoutin' for a change. I don't aim to let 'em get away with this."

The next day was Sunday, and the Hands went as usual to the old Cold Spring Church. The stares and whispers when Will walked in with his family were enough to make him chuckle inwardly. But he maintained the sober look that was expected of a good Presbyterian. At the end of the service, the minister gave him a searching glance as he shook his hand.

"Heard you were away, Willing," he said. "Glad to see you back."

The boys and young men crowded around him in the yard and listened in astonishment to his account of swimming ashore from the *Poictiers*. His cousin Abel got him alone afterward.

"Was that all true?" he asked, goggle-eyed. "Who took you prisoner?"

"The same pair o' British marines that came an' took Roger," Will told him. "They were hid out there at Leech's Tavern. They bound an' gagged us, an' about dark Ferd Leech led us to a boat on the south branch o' Fishin' Creek. Then they waited for night an' rowed out to the ship as smooth as you please. I'd never have gotten away if the *Poictiers* hadn't cleared for action. Did you see any o' the fight? It was a Yankee frigate that came down the bay."

Abel nodded. "I heard she was the *Wasp*. She outsailed the Britisher, an' they didn't try to follow her past Bombay Hook. Gee, Will—I'm awful sorry I wasn't more help!"

"Don't worry, Abel," Will answered. "We'll see that nest o' rattlesnakes cleaned out yet!"

When they reached home and he was helping his father unharness the mare, he laughed somewhat bitterly. "It's a funny thing," he said, "but when you tell most folks the truth, they don't want to believe you!"

"Never mind," the captain assured him. "We'll give 'em cause to believe the whole thing 'fore we get through!"

190

Eighteen

The late crops were ripening on the farm as October came in, and after his experience Will was quite content to stay at home and work. He carried a ladder out to the orchard and harvested many bushels of sound red apples. The pumpkins were ripe, too, and he brought in a wagonload, some almost as big as washtubs, to store in the root cellar. Then came the potato digging, hard work but gratifying when he turned up half a dozen fat tubers from a single hill.

While he busied himself with these chores, his father rode off on several mysterious errands. One day he was gone from dawn to sunset, and he told Will he had been all the way to Beesley's Point. There he found that the cargo of the Trinidad brig had been sold, and he rode home with his saddlebags heavy with money.

"Gosh, Dad," Will told him, "you were lucky nobody

robbed you! If the Leeches had any idea you were carryin' all that cash, I reckon they'd ha' been after you!"

Captain Hand smiled. "I was hopin' they would," he said. "Had a horse pistol all ready for 'em."

The next day he sent Will to the homes of all the crew members, telling them to come to the Hand farm that night. All of them showed up except Hannibal, who stayed on guard aboard the sloop.

"Well, boys," said the skipper, "I reckon you won't be needed again this fall unless somethin' special turns up. But the *Fair Molly* did pretty well as a privateer. Addin' it all together, the prizes brought in over thirty thousand dollars!"

He paused for the whistles and exclamations to die down, then went on. "I've figured out the shares, an' each one o' you gets eleven hundred an' twenty-five dollars. Double that for you, o' course, Amos. I've got the money wrapped separate for each of you, but I'd like you to count it an' make sure I'm correct."

For the next few minutes, the seamen pawed over their piles of bills and silver, their foreheads wrinkled with concentration, and finally all were satisfied. It was certainly more money than any of them had ever seen before.

"Beats fishin'," said Aaron Schellenger with a grin.

"Or buildin' road for the county," Matt Hughes commented.

Ezra Hand laughed. "Just be sure you take care of it," he advised. "You've got enough there to buy a good boat or some farmland."

At that point Will's mother and sisters came in, bearing

big pieces of spice cake and mugs of cider. Of course the party broke up on a jovial note.

"What do you figure Hannibal will do with his share?" Will asked when the crew had departed.

"Hard to say," the captain replied with a chuckle. "You know how independent he is about keepin' things to himself. But you can be sure he won't waste it in riotous livin'! What do you plan to do with your share?"

"Gosh!" said Will. "Funny, but I haven't thought about it. I guess the smartest thing would be to save the money till I really need it."

Early the next morning he asked his father if he might take the colt and ride to Dennis Creek. "I haven't had a chance to talk to Josh Townsend," he explained. "An' I've got some ideas about how to catch the Leeches spyin'. Besides, I've got a letter I want to mail, an' it'll go faster from up there."

His father pretended not to notice his red face. "Sure," he said. "Take the colt, an' welcome. I reckon it's important for that young lady to hear all about what you've been up to. But don't expect too much from Josh. He's got a lot o' militia business to 'tend to."

Will had an idea that stopping the spies was about as important as any militia business. He saddled Black Prince and rode off northward, on the Old Bay Road. He trotted the colt boldly past Leech's Tavern, but there was nobody about. He wouldn't have minded their seeing him, for he was sure the word of his escape must have reached them days before.

At Goshen he passed the mail coach, so he knew his

letter to Kate would be taken that day. When he got to Dennis, he went at once to the stage tavern that served as a post office and paid the charges for carrying the letter. Then, with a light heart, he rode to the militia encampment.

Lieutenant Townsend had a tent to himself, and an orderly took Will there after some questioning. Josh got up from the camp table where he was writing orders and shook Will's hand cordially.

"Believe me," he said, "I was glad to hear you were back home safe. I reckon you think I'm responsible for some of your troubles, and I can't say I blame you. But we had no way o' knowing what you were walking into. What can I do for you, Will?"

"It's the Leeches," said Will bluntly. "They're poison, an' you know it. Yet they're still goin' round free as air. An' I've got good reason to think that every move you make is passed on to the British from that tavern. Commodore Beresford as much as said so when he was questionin' me. We know they don't use lights to signal any more, but I think I know how to catch 'em dealin' with the enemy."

As he had hoped, the lieutenant showed immediate interest. "If that's really possible," he said, "I agree it's about the most important thing the militia can do. Want to tell me about your idea?"

"Could we go outside an' off by ourselves?" Will asked. "I'd like to talk where nobody can hear us."

Josh Townsend's face darkened for a moment, but then he consented. They strolled out of camp into an open field.

"You see," Will explained, "somebody seems to know all your plans. I didn't mean to accuse any o' your soldiers, but we may as well be sure. I reckon you heard about the boat the British brought right into the middle o' the county an' then smuggled me out the same way? Well, where they had it hid was only a little way from Leech's place. My guess is they send a boat ashore 'most every night, an' young Leech tells 'em what they want to know."

"That's hard for me to believe," said the lieutenant. "We've got watchers all along the bay shore, and they've spotted the boats that come in for water or to steal cattle just about every time."

"I know that," Will answered, "but remember those are big boats, full o' sailors an' red-coated marines. The ones I'm talkin' about are little skiffs, painted black, so they don't show much at night. An' the men in 'em wear home-spun. Once they're in the creek, anybody'd think they were nothin' but mushrat trappers or clammers. Besides, the tall reeds hide 'em most o' the time."

Townsend nodded slowly. "I believe you," he said. "Now, how do we catch young Leech in the act? That's what we need before we can make an arrest."

"I don't know," Will admitted, "unless you keep a tighter watch on the creeks an' tell your men what to look for. Maybe I can help if you let me."

"We could arrange that, I guess. I could put you on the rolls as a scout. Want to sign on now?"

Will hesitated. "Dunno's I could join the militia with-out talkin' to my dad first," he said. "He might need me on the sloop or for gettin' in the crops."

"All right, go home and ask him," the lieutenant told

him with a chuckle. "Meanwhile, I'll try to have extra guards posted along the shore."

On the way home, Will took the back roads, past lonely farms at the edge of the marshes. He wanted a closer look at some of the meandering tidal creeks, like the one down which he had been taken as a prisoner. There were almost more than he could count. First he crossed Beaver Swamp Creek, then a small unnamed stream that ran northwest into Dennis Creek, and then Goshen Creek. After that came Bidwell's Ditch and Dias Creek, each with several tributaries. A stretch of high ground came next, but he was soon in the area of Green Creek, followed by Fishing Creek. There were literally scores of hiding places for a meeting between a British landing party and a spy, though none were as close to Leech's Tavern as the one he remembered.

All he could do, he decided, was to count on the traitor using the same plan that had succeeded earlier. He had some doubts about his father's allowing him to join the militia, but perhaps the word "scout" would make the idea more palatable.

It was just past noon when he reached home again, and Ezra Hand had gone off somewhere on business. Will ate the dinner his mother had saved for him, then went out to the barn. He was standing there in the open barn door, thinking about his problem, when someone came walking up the lane. He looked twice before he recognized his old friend John Morris.

"Gosh!" said Will, "It's good to see you! But I thought you'd been called back to your ship."

"So I was," the lieutenant answered when they had shaken hands. "That was when the enemy fleet was expected to attack Philadelphia. But they sailed off to the south, so now I'm on special duty and back in Cape May County. I talked to some of your friends. What's this about your being a prisoner aboard the *Poictiers*?"

Will told Morris the story from the beginning, and the Navy man was keenly interested. He asked a number of questions about the great ship-of-the-line and was astonished to hear that Will had talked with Commodore Beresford.

"I reckon the only reason he'd speak to a common prisoner," said Will, "was to find out if Roger Thornhill was tellin' the truth. I backed him up, an' I hope he's a midshipman again."

"It was a great piece of luck for you that the *Wasp* showed up just when she did," Morris commented. "And I'd say you were mighty smart to take advantage of the call to quarters. The *Wasp* was just testing out the blockaders. Her captain knew he could outsail 'em, and of course he was safe enough once he got back to the protection of our shore batteries."

He heard from Will about the *Fair Molly's* prizes and was pleased to know that the crew had received so much money.

"Think your father plans to take her out again?" he asked.

"He hasn't said anything about it, an' from now on the autumn storms'll be coming along. Right now we want to catch that bunch o' traitors at Leech's Tavern."

"Well," said the lieutenant, "what's to stop you? After what they did to you, you certainly have the goods on 'em."

"Just my word against theirs," Will told him. "They say it wouldn't be enough to convict 'em. Treason's a pretty serious charge."

Morris looked thoughtful. "If you could use my help," he said after a moment, "I think it's the kind of job that would come under my orders."

"That would be great!" Will exclaimed. "You'd have the authority to make an arrest! All I can do alone, if I see anything wrong, is to go an' tell the militia."

"You're right," said Lieutenant Morris. "I believe I really can help. When do we start?"

"Soon as I've talked to Dad, I guess. He might have different ideas about it."

Just then they heard the thud of the mare's hoofs and the creak of wheels as the wagon turned in. Ezra Hand was warm in his welcome to the Navy officer.

"You goin' to be back with us a spell, John?" he asked.

"That depends. I'd like to lend a hand in catching these spies of yours, whoever they are. If it's all right with you, I'll work with Will."

The captain laughed. "No need to ask me," he said. "I reckon Will's earned the right to catch 'em if he can. Why don't you stay with us, John? We've got a spare bed now that Roger's gone."

To Will's delight, the lieutenant accepted. "It'll be a pleasure," Morris said. "I've been sleeping under haystacks the last couple of nights."

After supper he and Will went outside to talk over

plans for catching the spies. Will told him his theory that now that the light signals had stopped, boats from the fleet were coming ashore to get information. In the dirt of the dooryard, he drew a rough map with a stick.

"All these are creeks where the tide comes in," he explained. "Some of 'em run back a mile or more into the country. I figure the British are too smart to use the same one every time, but they know where the spy'll be waitin' to meet 'em each trip they make."

"Looks like a lot of area to cover," Morris observed. "How do you expect to be at the right place?"

"That's what Josh Townsend asked," said Will. "He's promised to put extra guards along the shore. But my idea would be to work from this end. I'm just about certain the spy is young Ferd Leech. So why not watch his place at night an' trail him when he leaves the tavern?"

Morris struck his fist into his palm. "Of course!" he said. "That's what we'll do. I'm ready to start tonight, if you are. First, though, I'd like to send a note to your Lieutenant Townsend. Let me talk to the skipper."

"Tonight's fine with me," Will assured him. "We'd better start for the tavern soon, though. It'll be dark in another hour, and I figure we should go afoot. Horses would just be in the way. I'm ready to go now if we've got everything we need."

Nineteen

Will and his companion set off within fifteen minutes, and as they left the lane, Ezra Hand rode past them on the black colt. He waved and trotted off up the road. It would be nearly four miles from the Hand farm to the tavern if they followed the highway. But Will knew short-cuts across the fields that would cut the distance to three miles. So he led the way through the October dusk, stepping along at a good pace.

They were both warmly clad, and their clothes were dark enough to be inconspicuous at night. Will carried his rifle, and Morris had a big Navy pistol. When they had been moving a little less than an hour, Will paused.

"The tavern's over yonder behind that little patch o' woods," he said. "There's two doors, and I figure he's more likely to use the back way instead o' comin' out in the road. So let's cross over right here an' get behind the buildin's.

Don't get too close because there's a little dog that barks at strangers. He's what got me in trouble that time they caught me."

They cut across the road out of sight of the inn and kept back in the woods the rest of the way. When they were a hundred yards from the place, Will held up a hand in caution. It was now almost completely dark, but through the cedar branches they could see dim candlelight coming from one of the rear windows.

As the minutes passed, Will began to have doubts. Perhaps young Leech had left for a rendezvous before they got there. Or, just as likely, there was no meeting with the British set for that night. He fidgeted a little, and Morris gripped his arm.

"Steady," he whispered. "You've got to have patience on this kind of job."

Will knew he was right. He concentrated on trying to remember the exact path his captors had taken the night he was caught. And while he was thinking about it, the back door of the tavern opened silently. For a second a shape appeared in the rectangle of light. Then the door closed again.

Will's heart began to beat faster, and he strained forward, trying to see where the figure went in the darkness. Morris's grip on his arm tightened, and Will saw him nod toward the left. They waited tensely for ten more seconds, then set off quietly in the same direction.

Experienced as he was in the woods, Will had a hard time matching the silent stride of his companion. The snap of a stick would give them away, but Morris moved like an

Indian through the brush. Will let him lead the way, trying to step where he had stepped.

This time, instead of heading west, the innkeeper's son was bearing more to the north. That meant he was making for the main channel of Fishing Creek rather than the south branch. His present course would bring him to the waterway a little below the village.

Morris halted, holding Will back. "He's stopped," the Navy man whispered. "He's looking around. Maybe he heard us."

But if Leech was suspicious, he must have decided he had been mistaken, for after a few seconds he went forward. Will could see him now, a stooped black shape, lean and wiry, moving along with knees bent.

They must be very close to the creek now. The woods had given way to low brush and tall, feathery marsh grass. Again Morris stopped Will and listened intently. Very faintly but not far ahead, they heard the sucking sound of a boot in wet mud. They waited, barely breathing. Will was grateful that the October night was too chilly for mosquitoes. Otherwise, the waiting would have been almost unbearable.

The minutes dragged by, and still they remained motionless. Then, suddenly and quite close ahead, a whippoorwill called, and Will felt a surge of excitement. No country boy would have been fooled by that whistle. It was Leech, signaling to someone.

Morris glanced back at him, and he nodded. Step by silent step they inched nearer until the hunched form of the spy appeared, crouching by the creek bank. Then from out of the shelter of the bulrushes, a small black boat came into view, and the dark figure on the bank straightened up.

"Leech?" growled a low voice from the boat. "Wot 'ave ye got for us tonight?"

"Quite a bit," a higher-pitched voice replied. "Only I want my money. Did you bring it with you?"

"Let's 'ear yer news first. Then we'll talk about money."

"All right—how's this? That Navy lieutenant from Philadelphia's back 'round here again. I think I know where he's stayin', too."

Will moved, bringing his rifle forward, but Morris checked him with a steady hand.

"Ah! An' ye've no idea wot 'is plans may be?"

"Not yet. But I'll find out. Now, what about my pay?"

"Bill," said the marine who had been speaking, "did the commodore send any money for the lad?"

"Aye," grunted the other man in the boat. "Five pound. 'E said there'd be more w'en we get solid information."

"Oh, I'll get it. Never fear!" Ferd whined. "Now gimme the five!"

The marine laughed. " 'Ere it is, boy—catch!" And he tossed a small bag that fell in the mud at Leech's feet.

It was then, while he scrambled for it, that Morris jumped forward. A blow from his pistol butt knocked out the innkeeper's son, and he faced the pair in the boat with the weapon cocked.

"Come on, Will," he said calmly. "If they try to get away, shoot 'em. All right, you two—out o' the boat! You're under arrest."

In the first instant, one of them had made a grab for the

oars, but the ring of authority in the lieutenant's voice
made him change his mind.

"March!" snapped Morris. "Take this traitor between
you and carry him!"

He stooped and picked up the purse, then followed the
prisoners, his pistol always at their backs. Will, meanwhile,
had pulled the boat up above the tide line and taken the
loaded musket that lay in the stern. Now he hurried to
overtake the little procession.

He offered the musket to the Navy man, but Morris told him to hold it ready and stay close.

"They know I can't miss with the pistol at this range," he said. "And even a British marine is no hero with a hole through his head."

Instead of going toward the tavern, the lieutenant headed his charges south to the place where he and Will had crossed the Bay Road. As they came out of the woods, Will stopped short in surprise. There in front of them, sitting their horses in the dim starlight, were five armed militiamen.

"It's all right, Will," said Morris with a chuckle. "I took a few precautions—that's why I sent the note from your place. Here you are, gentlemen. These are your spies. Take 'em and keep 'em well locked up. Lieutenant Townsend, if you'll come with us, I think we can give the senior Mr. Leech a little surprise."

Will recognized Josh Townsend then. The militia officer nodded to him as he dismounted.

"You ride my horse, Will," he said, "and we'll be right behind you on foot. Ride slowly up to the tavern door, as if you were a stranger looking for lodging. We'll keep out of sight while you talk to him."

As soon as Will had mounted Townsend's big bay, he turned up his coat collar and pulled his hat lower over his face. Then he rode on toward the inn at a walk. Before long he caught a glimpse of a light through the trees. There was a sandy driveway in front of the house, where the coaches pulled in.

"Whoa, there!" he said loudly to the horse. Then, without getting out of the saddle, he called, "Hello, the tavern! Anybody there?"

For a few seconds all was silent. Then the door opened a crack, and a querulous voice answered him.

"Who be ye?" asked the elder Leech. "What do ye want?"

Will tried to disguise his voice. "I've got a tired horse, an' I need a bed an' somethin' to eat," he replied in muffled tones.

"I dunno," said the innkeeper. "All our beds is full, an' the stable, too."

"I'll pay whatever it costs," Will told him. "I've got plenty o' money."

As he expected, the words had their effect on the greedy host.

"We-ell"—he hesitated—"maybe I can fix ye up. Have to charge ye two dollars, though."

"That's too high," said Will gruffly. "But I'll pay it. Now come an' take care o' my horse."

Ichabod Leech opened the door then and came down the two wooden steps toward the horse's head. It was just as he laid a hand on the bridle rein that Morris and Townsend stepped out of the darkness.

"You're under arrest, Leech," said the militiaman, "for treason against the United States of America."

"What!" screamed the tavern-keeper. "Where's my boy?"

"Well taken care of," Townsend answered. "He was caught, along with two men from the enemy fleet. Now we'll just take you to jail."

Leech snarled like a cornered rat, but Morris pinioned his arms, and he was finally taken away by Josh Townsend, his hands bound behind him. The militia lieutenant had remounted his horse and now rode off beside his sullen prisoner.

"Tired, Will?" asked John Morris. "I'll be ready to tumble into that spare bed by the time we get to your house."

"Gee," Will told him, "I must ha' been too excited to notice, but I guess I'll be ready for bed myself. What time you reckon it is?"

"Only a bit after ten o'clock, I'd say. Things happened fast, once they started. But don't forget we've got to walk home. Let's be on our way."

*　　*　　*

The Hand family were all asleep when Will and the Navy lieutenant reached the house. But the bed in the front room had been turned down, ready for the guest. In the morning Will was roused by sounds from the kitchen and came down in time for breakfast, but he found John Morris was there before him. Then his father came in from doing the early chores, and the three of them sat down at the table.

"Your turn to say grace, son," said Ezra Hand.

Will gave thanks as usual for their food and well-being, but he wound up his prayer in a different way. "And thank Thee, Lord," he concluded, "for delivering the traitors an' the enemy into our hands."

His father looked up and frowned at him. "What's this?" he asked. "Are you bein' funny, or are you serious?"

"Serious, Dad. Lieutenant, why don't you tell him?"

So, as they ate, Morris gave the details of their evening's adventure. "You've got Will to thank," he said. "It was his idea. But as you know, I'd already fixed things up with Townsend to have some men handy near the tavern. So everything went smooth as silk. They took both the Leeches to the county jail in Middle Town."

"Well, I'll be hornswoggled!" was all Captain Hand could say. "Quite a night you boys had! You stayin' down here for a spell, Lieutenant?"

"I'll have to testify at the trial," Morris replied. "But I think they'll hold a special session of court in this case. We've certainly got all the evidence we need, so it shouldn't take long. As a matter o' fact, my assignment down here was to help clean up this spy business. I have a feeling the war may not last too much longer. The British are finding us a hard nut to crack."

"Thank goodness!" Martha Hand put in. "You really have good reasons for thinking it's near the end?"

"Well, the redcoats were defeated down at Baltimore, and they must know they can't take New York or Philadelphia. The blockade's successful enough, but it's tying up a lot of their ships and men. They're short of food and water, too. What I look for now is a big attack on the Gulf ports—most likely New Orleans."

He finished his coffee and turned to the captain. "What about the *Fair Molly*?" he asked. "Do you plan on another privateering cruise?"

Ezra Hand shook his head. "We've had plenty o' luck up to now, but I don't want to push it too far. Reckon I'll wait an' see if the war ends, as you say. Then I can go back to pilotin'."

Will looked disappointed. "Shucks!" he said. "I was gettin' to like it. Just the same, I guess everybody'd rather have peace."

"Amen!" said his mother devoutly.

When John Morris accompanied Will out to the barn, he gave him a few words of advice.

"I know how you love the sea," said the lieutenant. "If your father goes back to piloting, I suppose he'll need you to help with the sloop. But did you ever think about the Navy as a career?"

"Reckon I don't have enough schoolin' to be an officer," Will answered regretfully. "I suppose I could join up as a seaman, though."

"How much education have you had, Will?"

" 'Bout six winters in the Lower Township Common School. They teach you to read an' write an' cipher, an' a little about history an' geography."

"But you never worked very hard at it, did you?"

"No, I guess not," Will admitted sheepishly.

"Too bad," Morris told him. "Because I think you're a bright lad. With just a bit more learning and the money to pay for it, I believe you could go on to college. Then a Navy commission wouldn't be hard to get. But come on, we've got chores to do."

            ❖   ❖   ❖

Two or three days later, when Will was shucking corn in the field, he saw a rider enter the dooryard. Looking more closely, he saw it was Aaron Schellenger, and he waved and shouted to him to come on over. As Aaron rode up, he was holding a letter in his hand.

"This came by the Cape May stage," he called. "Must be important. It's addressed to Willing Hand, Esq. Never knew you was a squire, Will."

Will took the letter in his work-stained fingers and looked at it. A sheet of fine writing paper had been neatly folded and sealed with wax. The address was written in a bold, round hand that he had never seen before. Yet he knew who must have written it without breaking the seal.

"Thank you, Aaron," he said, trying to hide his blushes. "I'll read it soon as I go in," and he tucked the letter carefully into his linsey-woolsey shirt.

"It's near noon," said Aaron, "an' I thought I might have dinner with you. Come on along, now. I want to hear all about how you caught those dirty Leeches."

So it was another full hour before Will could get to his room and open the letter in privacy.

"My dear Will," it read. "How very exciting your life must be these days! I was thrilled to hear that the same *Fair Molly* in which we sailed to Cape May had been victorious in battle! I expect you will be quite rich after all the prizes you've taken. Here in the city it has been a dull time. Parties and picnics, of course, but now I'm back in Miss Horsham's School, and all such pleasures are over. Please write to me again, dear Will, and tell about your further adventures. It will help to pass the long months until I see you again at my beloved Cape Island.

"Your faithful friend,

"Kate Perry"

Twenty

When the one-room school on Tabernacle Road opened for the winter term, Will was there. It was a little frame building with hand-hewn oak timbers and vertical cedar siding. The floor was of broad pine planks, and the benches were pegged to the floor so that they couldn't be moved. Twenty-four pupils were present, ranging in age from five-year-olds to big boys and girls well along in their teens. The teacher was the same bespectacled young man who had been there the year before. He seemed surprised when Will came up to the desk after classes were over.

"Yes, Willing?" he said. "Something you wanted to ask?"

"Mr. Dawson, sir, would you say I was a good student?"

"Ahem!" The teacher hesitated. "I think you have intelligence, but I've never seen you make much effort. I fear the answer would have to be no."

"All right," Will told him. "I guess you're right. But this year I want to learn—learn all you can teach me. I want to learn things like algebra and geometry, an' how to talk right. Could you lend me some books maybe an' help me understand 'em?"

Mr. Dawson's pale face lit up. "If you really mean it, nothing would make me happier!" he said.

"You see," Will explained, "I want to go to college, an' I know I need a lot more schoolin'."

Again the teacher showed his delight. "I truly believe," he said, "if you have that attitude, I could get you ready for Princeton in a year's time!"

And Will, fired with zeal and determination, went to work on his studies as he never had before.

The corn was in the barn now, and all the autumn farm tasks were finished. When John Morris found that the county judge would be away for a month and the special court session had to be postponed, he went back to Philadelphia. Before leaving he had a word with Will.

"I'm mighty pleased at the way you're taking hold of your school work," he said. "Keep at it! And as soon as I'm notified, I'll be back for the trial. I'll see you then."

By the middle of November, Will could tell that his father was getting fidgety. There was firewood to be cut and hauled and other winter chores to be done, but the captain's heart was with his sloop. He even talked of taking her out privateering again, but Martha Hand finally discouraged him in that idea.

"Ezra," she said, "you've made a lot o' money. 'Cordin' to county standards, you're a rich man. What's the good o' riskin' it all—an' maybe your neck—on another venture? When you get the itch to go to sea, think about your family."

Cold weather had set in early, and there was ice in the bays and inlets. Also the men of the crew had drifted off to other jobs, and Will was too wrapped up in getting an education to be of any use as a seaman. So, grudgingly, the captain contented himself with spending all his spare time with Hannibal, in the snug cabin of the *Fair Molly*, waiting for the war to end.

On a bitter day in December, word came from Middle Town that court would be convened the Monday after Christmas. Knowing John Morris's habits, Will wasn't surprised when he appeared at the door that Sunday morning. But this time, instead of his usual homespun garb, he had on his lieutenant's uniform under a blue Navy greatcoat. He went to church with the Hand family and spent the night at their house, riding up the sandy road in the wagon with Will and his father on Monday.

The courthouse was a simple, white-painted frame building that would seat perhaps fifty people, and every bench was filled. The proceedings were given dignity by the presence of Judge Corson and Sheriff Leaming, two of Cape May County's most distinguished men.

The Leeches, father and son, were brought into court and pleaded not guilty. They were defended by a Cumberland County lawyer named Githens, who gave an impassioned opening address to the jury of farmers. How, he asked, could anyone seriously consider the grave charge of treason, when applied to a pair of such quiet, well-behaved, outstanding citizens?

The prosecution went about its business with less fanfare, but the evidence was too strong to leave any doubts. Josh Townsend, the first witness, told how the militia had tried for a year to find how information was being given to the British. Then he described the signal lights on the bluff, answered from the fleet.

Abel Hand followed him on the stand. He blushed and stammered over his own part in the affair, but he did establish the fact that Will had gone to spy on the tavern and hadn't come back.

Then it was Will's own turn. He told his story briefly and well, from the time he had been knocked out and placed in the tavern cellar to his escape from the *Poictiers*. The defense attorney tried hard to shake his testimony, but he stuck to the simple truth.

The final witness for the state was John Morris, impressive in his Navy blues. And after telling how Ferd Leech had met the skiff bearing the enemy marines, he clinched it by mentioning the payment made to the innkeeper's son. The little bag holding the five English pounds was identified by Will and the militiamen, and the prosecution rested its case.

The defense brought two stage drivers to testify to the good character of the Leeches, but they made poor witnesses. So the case went to the jury. They were out less than an hour and brought in a verdict of guilty against both Ichabod and Ferdinand Leech, recommending life imprisonment rather than hanging. And Judge Corson accepted the recommendation when he imposed sentence.

Thus Leech's Tavern went out of business, and the enemy ships in Delaware Bay were no longer able to know American plans in advance.

*   *   *

Two weeks after the trial ended, disturbing news reached the people of the cape. Commodore Stephen

Decatur, tired of staying bottled up with his ships in New York Harbor, had come out to fight. His flagship, the *President*, was captured, and he became a British prisoner. Decatur had always been a hero in the county, especially at Cape Island. A pall of gloom hung over them all.

Most of their unhappiness was chased away at the end of January, however, when news came of General Jackson's great victory at New Orleans. And within a few more weeks they heard that peace had been declared! Actually, of course, the Treaty of Paris had been signed the day before Christmas, but sailing ships had to fight head winds on the Atlantic in winter, so news was slow.

All prisoners of war were soon exchanged. Will had wondered about the black seamen from the *Carlotta* and what would happen to them. He was glad to hear that they had escaped from the stockade some time earlier, and nobody knew where they had gone. One thing seemed sure—they would never be slaves again.

The winter term at Lower Township School ended at Easter, in time for the spring plowing. But brief as it was, Will had made amazing progress. He had worked hard all winter, and Mr. Dawson gave him high marks, not only for effort but also for achievement. He was ready, the schoolmaster said, to take the examinations for Princeton.

Ezra Hand grumbled a little at the prospect of his son's going to college, but when Will had taken the examinations, passed them, and been accepted, his father was secretly proud of him.

"Reckon you can go on to big things," the captain admitted. "But I'm sure goin' to lose a good foremast hand!"

"Not yet," Will told him. "We've got all summer, and I'm ready to sail with the sloop whenever you are."

They careened the *Fair Molly* that spring, scraped her hull, and gave her a fresh coat of paint. In late April they sailed for Philadelphia, carrying a cargo of pork and beef from nearby farms.

The chain booms were gone from the upper river, and there were big square-rigged merchant ships making sail for Europe, China, and the West Indies. Ezra Hand looked them over with interest.

"Reckon it's time I went back to pilotin'," he told his son. "All the ships'll be makin' voyages now, an' they'll need pilots below Bombay Hook. I'm afraid the packet sloops are about finished anyhow. They're buildin' steamboats that'll make the trip to Cape May in one day 'stead o' two."

Will knew his father was right. He had loved the voyages to the city and back, but steam was bound to take the place of sail in sheltered waters. Perhaps, he thought, by the time he was out of college and in the Navy, there would even be warships with steam engines!

They sold their cargo to the Dock Street merchants. Then the captain went to the headquarters of the Delaware River and Bay Pilots, on Walnut Street. While he was there, Will watched the fine ladies going in and out of the shops, discussing styles and prices. At last, he told himself with a chuckle, he would be able to tell his sisters what fashionable women were wearing.

Ezra Hand came out smiling. "License is all in order," he told Will. "An' they need pilots so bad, the rates are up.

So we'll make a good livin', summer an' winter. An' the *Fair Molly* can go back to doin' what she was built for."

They went back aboard, ready for one of Hannibal's famous chowders. And when the tide turned, they set sail for home. Will looked up at the sloop's lofty mast and the smooth set of her mainsail with real affection.

"Quite a life you've led, for a little old Cape May lady," he mused. "Pilot boat, bucking those tides and rips off the Delaware Capes. Then a market packet on the bay, with good food and berths for tourists. And after that a fighting privateer—terror of British coastwise shipping. Now, I guess, you'll be sort of glad to get back to your rightful job. I'll help sail you all summer, old girl. But when I have to go off to college in the fall—golly, how I'll miss you!"